國家圖書館出版品預行編目資料

跟老外介紹台灣這本全包了 / 張文娟著-- 初版.
-- 新北市：雅典文化事業有限公司, 民114.03
　　面；　公分. --（全民學英文；72）
　　ISBN 978-626-7245-65-1（平裝）

1. CST: 英語 2. CST: 旅遊 3. CST: 讀本
805.18　　　　　　　　　　113020238

全民學英文系列 72

跟老外介紹台灣這本全包了

著／張文娟
責任編輯／張瑜凌
美術編輯／鄭孝儀
封面設計／不恬黃

掃描填回函
好書隨時抽

法律顧問：方圓法律事務所／涂成樞律師

總經銷：永續圖書有限公司

www.foreverbooks.com.tw

出版日／2025年03月

雅典文化

出版社　22103 新北市汐止區大同路三段194號9樓之1
　　　　　　TEL　（02）8647-3663
　　　　　　FAX　（02）8647-3660

版權所有，任何形式之翻印，均屬侵權行為

◎第3組—結合子音規則

【ch】去 -chair 椅子	【sh】噓 -share 分享	【gh】個 -ghost 鬼
【ph】夫 -phone 電話	【wh】或 -what 什麼	【rh】若 -rhino 犀牛
【th】思 -thin 瘦的 (伸出舌頭，無聲)	【th】日 -that 那個 (伸出舌頭，有聲)	【bl】貝樂 -black 黑的
【cl】克樂 -class 班級	【fl】夫樂 -flower 花朵	【gl】個樂 -glass 玻璃
【pl】配樂 -play 玩耍	【sl】思樂 -slow 慢的	【br】貝兒 -break 打破
【cr】擴兒 -cross 橫越	【dr】桌兒 -dream 夢	【fr】佛兒 -free 自由的
【gr】過兒 -great 優秀的	【pr】配兒 -pray 祈禱	【tr】綽兒 -train 火車
【wr】若 -write 寫字	【kn】呢 -know 知道	【mb】嗯(閉嘴) -comb 梳子
【ng】嗯(張嘴) -sing 唱歌	【tch】去 -catch 捉住	【sk】思個 -skin 皮膚
【sm】思麼 -smart 聰明	【sn】思呢 -snow 雪	【st】思的 -stop 停止
【sp】思貝 -speak 說話	【sw】思握 -sweater 毛衣	

track 跨頁共同導讀 000

◎第4組─結合母音規則

【ai】 欸意 -rain 雨水	【ay】 欸意 -way 方式	【aw】 歐 -saw 鋸子
【au】 歐 -sauce 醬汁	【ea】 意 -seat 座位	【ee】 意 -see 看見
【ei】 欸意 -eight 八	【ey】 欸意 -they 他們	【ew】 物 -new 新的
【ie】 意 -piece 一片	【oa】 歐 -boat 船	【oi】 喔意 -oil 油
【oo】 物 -food 食物	【ou】 澳 -outside 外面	【ow】 歐 -grow 成長
【oy】 喔意 -boy 男孩	【ue】 物 -glue 膠水	【ui】 物 -fruit 水果
【a_e】 欸意 -game 遊戲	【e_e】 意 -delete 刪除	【i_e】 愛 -side 邊、面
【o_e】 歐 -hope 希望	【u_e】 物 -use 使用	【ci】 思 -circle 圓圈
【ce】 思 -center 中心	【cy】 思 -cycle 循環	【gi】 句 -giant 巨人
【ge】 句 -gentle 溫和的	【gy】 句 -gym 體育館	【ar】 啊兒 -far 遠的
【er】 兒 -enter 輸入	【ir】 兒 -bird 小鳥	【or】 歐兒 -order 順序
【ur】 兒 -burn 燃燒	【igh】 愛 -high 高的	【ind】 愛嗯的 -find 找到

※ 小試身手：

現在你可以運用上述自然發音的規則，試念以下這些句子：

★ Anything wrong?

★ It's time for bed.

★ Let's go for a ride.

★ May I use the phone?

★ Nice to meet you.

★ That sounds good.

★ I feel thirsty.

★ Turn off the light, please.

★ May I leave now?

★ Here you are.

Unit 1 — First Contact 第一次接觸

- Unit 1 May I help you? 需要我幫忙嗎？..............017
- Unit 2 What's your name? 你叫什麼名字？..........021
- Unit 3 Where are you from? 你是哪國人？..........025
- Unit 4 Do you speak Chinese? 你會說中文嗎？...029
- Unit 5 Are you a backpacker? 你是背包客嗎？....034
- Unit 6 Self Introduction 自我介紹......................038
- Unit 7 Let me show you around in Taiwan. 讓我帶你遊台灣。..................................042

Unit 2 — Tourist Spots in Taipei 台北觀光景點

- Unit 1 National Palace Museum 國立故宮博物院 ..047
- Unit 2 National Chiang Kai-shek Memorial Hall 國立中正紀念堂...052
- Unit 3 National Theater and Concert Hall 國家戲劇院和音樂廳..................................057
- Unit 4 Sun Yat-sen Memorial Hall 國父紀念館.....062
- Unit 5 Taipei 101 台北 101...................................067
- Unit 6 National Historical Museum 國立歷史博物館.......................................072
- Unit 7 Beitou 北投...076
- Unit 8 Maokong 貓空..081

Unit 3 Northern Scenic Spots 北部風景區

Unit 1 Keelung 基隆 085
Unit 2 Jiufen 九份 089
Unit 3 Wulai 烏來 093
Unit 4 Tamsui 淡水 098
Unit 5 Yingge 鶯歌 103
Unit 6 Sanxia 三峽 107
Unit 7 Bitan Scenic Area 碧潭風景區 112
Unit 8 Daxi 大溪 116
Unit 9 Jiaoxi 礁溪 120

Unit 4 Central Scenic Spots 中部風景區

Unit 1 Sanyi Township 三義鄉 125
Unit 2 Dajia Zhenlan Temple 大甲鎮瀾宮 129
Unit 3 Lugang 鹿港 133
Unit 4 Baguashan Giant Buddha Scenic Area
八卦山大佛風景區 137
Unit 5 Sun Moon Lake 日月潭 141
Unit 6 Xitou 溪頭 145
Unit7 Qingjing Farm 清境農場 149
Unit 8 Aowanda National Forest Recreation Area
奧萬大國家森林遊樂區 153

Unit 5　Southern Scenic Spots
南部風景區

Unit 1　Alishan　阿里山 157
Unit 2　Anping District, Tainan City　臺南安平.....161
Unit 3　Tainan Confucius Temple　臺南孔廟 165
Unit 4　The Love River　愛河 169
Unit 5　Qijin　旗津 173
Unit 6　Xizi Bay　西子灣 177
Unit 7　Kenting　墾丁 181

Unit 6　Eastern Scenic Spots
東部風景區

Unit 1　Taroko Gorge　太魯閣峽谷 185
Unit 2　Carp Lake　鯉魚潭 189
Unit 3　Hualien City　花蓮市 193
Unit 4　Xiuguluan River　秀姑巒溪....................197
Unit 5　Ruisui　瑞穗 201
Unit 6　Zhiben Hot Spring　知本溫泉 205
Unit 7　Sanxiantai　三仙台 209

Unit 7 Offshore Islands 離島

Unit 1 Introduction to Orchid Island 介紹蘭嶼 ... 213
Unit 2 A Tour on Orchid Island 參觀蘭嶼 217
Unit 3 Indigenous People: the Tao tribe
原住民：達悟族 221
Unit 4 Green Island 綠島 225
Unit 5 Matzu 馬祖 229
Unit 6 Kinmen 金門 233
Unit 7 Penghu 澎湖 237

Unit 8 Night Markets 夜市

Unit 1 Introduction to Shilin Night Market
介紹士林夜市 241
Unit 2 Shilin Night Market Food
士林夜市美食 245
Unit 3 Shopping at Shilin Night Market
於士林夜市購物 249
Unit 4 Local Products 當地產品 253
Unit 5 Guest Feedback 客人意見 257
Unit 6 Famous Night Markets in Taiwan.
台灣各大知名夜市 261

Unit 9 Temples 佛寺廟宇

Unit 1 Introduction to Fo Guang Shan
　　　　介紹佛光山..................................265
Unit 2 A Tour in Fo Guang Shan　參觀佛光山.....269
Unit 3 Buddha Memorial Center　佛陀紀念館.....273
Unit 4 One Day Life in the Temple　佛門的一天.277
Unit 5 Learning Meditation　學習靜坐.................281
Unit 6 After the Visit to Fo Guang Shan
　　　　參觀佛光山後心得..................................285
Unit 7 Famous Buddhist Temples in Taiwan
　　　　台灣各大佛寺。.......................................289

Unit 10 Festivals 節日

Unit 1 The Lunar New Year　農曆新年................293
Unit 2 The Lantern Festival　元宵節....................297
Unit 3 Tomb Sweeping Day　清明節...................301
Unit 4 The Dragon Boat Festival　端午節............305
Unit 5 Chinese Valentine's Day　七夕情人節......309
Unit 6 Hungry Ghost Festival　中元節.................313
Unit 7 Mid-Autumn Festival　中秋節..................317

TAIWAN Let's Go!

Unit 11 Health Trip 健康之旅

Unit 1 Tai Chi 太極拳 321
Unit 2 Qi Gong 氣功 325
Unit 3 Yoga 瑜珈 329
Unit 4 Spa 水療 333
Unit 5 Chinese Medicine 中醫 337
Unit 6 Massage 按摩 341

Unit 12 Returning 回國

Unit 1 Checking out of the Hotel 飯店退房 345
Unit 2 Buying Souvenirs 買紀念品 349
Unit 3 Expressing Gratitude 感謝 353
Unit 4 Final Farewells 最後道別 357

Chapter 1

First Contact
第一次接觸

 002 track

Unit 1

May I help you?
需要我幫忙嗎?

● 情境對話 1

A May I help you?
需要我幫忙嗎?

B Yes, I am looking for Dihua Street on this map.
需要,我正在地圖上找迪化街。

A Just go straight and turn left and you'll find Dihua Street.
向前直走再左轉就可以看到迪化街了。

B I see. Thank you.
我明白了。謝謝。

A In fact, I am going to that street, too. I can take you there.
事實上,我也要到那裡去。我可以帶你去。

B That's great. Thank you.
太好了。謝謝。

track 跨頁共同導讀 002

情境對話 2

A Do you need any help?
你需要我幫忙嗎?

B Yes, I think I got lost.
需要,我想我迷路了。

A Where are you going?
你要到哪裡去?

B I was going to meet my friends on Dihua Street.
我要到迪化街去和我朋友碰面。

A It's not far from here. If you keep walking, you can see Dihua Street on the left.
那兒離這裡不遠。如果你直走下去,就可以在你左邊看到迪化街。

B Thank you very much.
真謝謝你。

A I am going to Dihua Street to do some shopping.
Why don't you go with me?
我正要去迪化街購物,你何不和我一起去?

B That's very kind of you.
你真是好心。

TAIWAN
Let's Go!

003 track

ⒶA常說的話●

May I help you?
需要我幫忙嗎?

Do you need any help?
你需要我幫忙嗎?

You seem to be lost. Where are you going?
你看來好像迷路了。你要到哪裡去?

Where would you like to go?
你想要上哪兒?

Go straight until you come to the post office.
一直向前走到郵局。

Take the second right and you'll see Dihua Street.
在第二個路口右轉,你就會看見迪化街。

At the traffic lights, turn right into Dihua Street.
在紅綠燈那裡,向右轉入迪化街。

It's the third street on your left.
在你左邊的第三條街就是了。

track 跨頁共同導讀 003

Ⓑ常說的話

Excuse me, can you help me? I am lost!
不好意思,你能幫幫我嗎?我迷路了!

I'd like to go to Dihua Street, but I can't find it.
Is it close here?
我想要去迪化街,但是我找不到在哪兒。
它離這裡近嗎?

Could you tell me where Dihua Street is?
你能告訴我迪化街在哪兒嗎?

Can you tell me how to get to Dihua Street?
你能告訴我要怎樣才能到迪化街嗎?

How do I get to Dihua Street from here?
從這裡要怎樣才能到迪化街?

How do you get to Dihua Street?
要怎樣才能到迪化街?

Could you give me directions to Dihua Street?
你能告訴我到迪化街該怎麼走嗎?

What's the best way to get to Dihua Street?
從這裡到迪化街怎麼走最快?

 004 track

第一次接觸

Unit 2 What's your name?
你叫什麼名字?

● 情境對話 1

A What's your name?
你叫什麼名字?

B My name is Amy.
我的名字叫愛咪。

A That's a nice name.
很不錯的名字。

B What about you?
那你呢?

A I am Wendy.
我叫溫蒂。

B Nice to meet you, Wendy.
溫蒂,很高興認識你。

track 跨頁共同導讀 004

●情境對話2

Ⓐ May I have your name?
方便告訴我你的名字嗎?

Ⓑ You can call me Amy. What is your name?
你可以叫我愛咪。你叫什麼名字呢?

Ⓐ My English name is Wendy.
我的英文名字叫溫蒂。

Ⓑ What is your Chinese name then?
那你的中文名字叫什麼?

Ⓐ My Chinese name is Wei-hui.
我的中文名字叫偉慧。

Ⓑ That sounds very nice. Does it have a meaning?
聽起來很好聽。這名字有什麼意義嗎?

Ⓐ Thank you. It means great wisdom.
謝謝。這名字的意思是「偉大的智慧」。

Ⓑ I love Chinese names with meanings.
我喜歡有意義的中文名字。

ⒶⒸ常說的話●

What is your name?
你叫什麼名字？

May I have your name?
方便告訴我你的名字嗎？

How shall I address you?
我該怎麼稱呼你？

What is your last name/ family name/ surname?
你貴姓？

What is your first name/ given name/ Christian name?
你叫什麼名字？

Do you have a Chinese name?
你有中文名字嗎？

What does your first name mean?
你的名字有什麼意義？

Is that an Irish last name?
那是個愛爾蘭的姓氏嗎？

track 跨頁共同導讀 005

Ⓑ 常說的話●

My name is Amy.
我的名字叫愛咪。

You can call me Amy.
你可以叫我愛咪。

You can call me Miss Brown.
你可以稱我布朗小姐。

I am called Amy Brown.
我叫愛咪布朗。

Amy is my first name, and Brown is my last name.
我的名字叫愛咪,我姓布朗。

I have a Chinese name, Ai-mei.
我有個中文名字叫愛美。

I don't have a Chinese name yet.
我還沒有中文名字。

What is the meaning of your first name?
你的名字的意義是什麼?

 006 track

Unit 3 Where are you from?
你是哪國人？

● 情境對話 1 ●

A Where are you from?
你是哪國人？

B I am from the United States.
我來自美國。

A You are American then.
那麼你就是美國人了。

B Yes, and you? Are you from Taiwan?
是的，那你呢？你是台灣人嗎？

A That's right. I'm Taiwanese.
對，我是台灣人。

B Then you are my first Taiwanese friend.
那麼你就是我的第一個台灣朋友。

track 跨頁共同導讀 006

●情境對話2

Ⓐ What's your nationality?
你的國籍是?

Ⓑ American. I am from Seattle.
美國。我來自西雅圖。

Ⓐ I was born in Taipei, so I am Taiwanese.
我是在台北出生的,所以我是台灣人。

Ⓑ I am glad to make a Taiwanese friend finally.
真高興終於認識了一位台灣朋友。

Ⓐ The pleasure is mine.
是我的榮幸。

Ⓑ Can you speak Taiwanese?
你會說台語嗎?

Ⓐ Yes, I speak fluent Taiwanese.
會,我的台語很流利。

Ⓑ I'm going to need your help a lot during my stay here.
在這裡的期間,我會非常需要你的幫忙。

Ⓐ常說的話

Where are you from?
你是哪國人?

Which country do you come from?
你來自哪個國家?

Which state of America are you from?
你來自美國的哪一州?

What is your nationality?
你的國籍是?

Are you an American or a Canadian?
你是美國人還是加拿大人?

What languages do you speak?
你會說哪些語言?

Are you an English native speaker?
你是英語母語者嗎?

You look a little like Taiwanese.
Is one of your parents from Taiwan?
你看來有點像台灣人,你的父母當中有人是台灣人嗎?

track 跨頁共同導讀 007

Ⓑ 常說的話

I am from the U.S.A.
我來自美國。

I am from Seattle, a city of the Northwestern United States.
我來自西雅圖,美國西北部的一個城市。

I am from Canada, not America.
我來自加拿大,不是美國。

I am an English native speaker.
我是英語母語者。

Have you ever been to the United States?
你去過美國嗎?

Are you a local Taiwanese?
你是台灣當地人嗎?

Can you understand Taiwanese?
你聽得懂台語嗎?

Your English is very good. Where did you learn English?
你的英語非常好。你是在哪裡學英語的?

 008 track

Unit 4 Do you speak Chinese?
你會說中文嗎？

● 情境對話 1

A Do you speak Chinese?
你會說中文嗎？

B No, I can't speak Chinese.
我不會說中文。

A Are you going to learn Chinese?
你要開始學中文嗎？

B I'd like to, but I am afraid it would be very hard for me.
我很想，但是我怕中文對我來說很難學。

A Don't worry about it because I can help you with that.
這你不用煩惱，因為我會幫你。

B I am sure you can be of great help.
我相信你能幫我這個大忙。

track 跨頁共同導讀 009

I can help you with Chinese conversation, but I can't do your homework for you.
我可以幫你練習對話,但我不能替你做家庭作業。

You can make friends with Taiwanese much more easily if you learn a little bit of Chinese.
如果你學了一點中文,要交台灣朋友會更容易些。

Ⓑ常說的話

I've only picked up some Chinese phrases here and there.
我只有隨便學了點中文用法。

Learning how to write Chinese characters seems to be impossible for me now.
現在我覺得要我學寫中文字,看來不太可能。

I'll learn to have a simple conversation in Chinese first.
首先我會學怎麼說中文的簡單會話。

Most Taiwanese speak English very well, and there is no need for me to learn Chinese.
大部分的台灣人英語說得很好,我沒必要學中文。

That is really very kind of you to be willing to practice Chinese with me.
你人真好,願意和我練習中文。

If I could order a table of food in Chinese, I would be very proud of myself.
要是我能用中文點一桌的菜,我會非常自以為傲。

Some Taiwanese speak only Taiwanese here, and I can't understand it at all.
這兒有些人只說台語,我完全沒辦法聽懂。

I can communicate with most Taiwanese with my body language.
我可以靠肢體語言和大部分台灣人溝通。

 track 010

Unit 5 Are you a backpacker?
你是背包客嗎?

● 情境對話 1 ●

A Why are you coming to Taiwan?
你為何來台灣?

B I came here to travel around.
我來這兒到處旅行。

A What would you like to see in Taiwan?
你想要看那些事物呢?

B I am very interested in mountain climbing and camping.
我對登山和露營感興趣。

A Are you going to travel alone as a backpacker?
你要當背包客,一個人旅遊嗎?

B Yes, I have been a backpacker many times.
對,我當背包客好幾次了。

010 track 跨頁共同導讀

情境對話 2

A What's your purpose of coming to Taiwan?
你來台灣的目的是？

B I'd like to backpack in Taiwan for a while.
我想要當背包客，單獨遊台灣一陣子。

A Where do you plan to go in Taiwan?
你計畫到台灣哪兒呢？

B I'd like to do some outdoor activities, such as mountain climbing and camping.
我想要從事戶外活動，像是登山和露營。

A If that's the case, you have come to the right country.
那麼你來對國家了。

B I've read some guidebooks on traveling in Taiwan.
我讀了些關於在台灣旅行的導遊書。

A There are many beautiful mountains and scenic spots here.
這兒有很多美麗的山岳和景點。

B Right now, I am ready to begin my exploration.
現在我已經準備好要開始我的探險了。

 track 011

Ⓐ 常說的話

Are you going to backpack alone in Taiwan?
你要當背包客,單獨遊台灣?

Do you feel safe as a female backpacker traveling alone?
當女性背包客,單獨旅遊,你感到安全嗎?

What if you can't solve some problems by yourself?
要是你沒辦法獨自解決某些問題怎麼辦?

Are you going to set up a tent and stay there overnight alone?
你要在那兒搭帳篷,獨自過夜?

Wouldn't your parents back home worry very much for you?
難道你家鄉的父母不會很擔心你?

You don't even speak Chinese; how are you going to communicate with the locals?
你連中文都不會說,你要怎樣和當地人溝通?

Do you have people in Taiwan you can contact in case of emergency?
你在台灣有緊急聯絡人嗎?

In case you have an emergency, please dial 119.
要是你有緊急狀況,請撥打 119。

Ⓑ常說的話

I've backpacked in many countries by myself.
我曾經在很多國家當背包客,獨自旅行過。

In my home country, many young people backpack alone in a foreign country, including females.
在我們國家,很多年輕人會去國外當背包客,獨自旅行,包括女性。

Most local Taiwanese are very friendly, and they can speak English.
大部分台灣當地人都非常和善,又會說英語。

To get away from people is the main purpose of backpacking.
當背包客主要目的就是要遠離人群。

Usually there are many other backpackers going to the same destinations.
通常有很多其他背包客要到同一個目的地。

It is easy to make friends with other backpackers because they can help each other.
因為背包客會互相幫忙,所以他們常成為朋友。

As soon as I get back to the city from backpacking, I'll let you know.
當我背包客旅行一結束,回到城裡,就會聯絡你。

I bought travel insurance before leaving my home country.
在離開我的國家前,我投保了旅遊險。

track 012

Unit 6 Self Introduction
自我介紹

情境對話 1

A Are you a college student?
你是個大學生嗎?

B Yes, I am having my summer vacation now.
對,我現在放暑假。

A What about you? Are you a college student, too?
那你呢?你也是個大學生嗎?

B I graduated from a university last year, and I am working now.
我去年剛從大學畢業,現在我在工作。

A What do you do?
你是從事哪一行的?

B I am a secretary in a trading company.
我現在在一家貿易公司當秘書。

012 track 跨頁共同導讀

● 情境對話2

A Are you a college student on summer vacation?
你是個放暑假的大學生嗎?

B Yes, I'm going to become a graduate student.
對,我升上去是個研究生。

A What do you major in?
你主修什麼?

B I study Information Technology Management.
我主修資訊管理。

A You will find a job easily after you graduate.
你畢業後要找工作很容易。

B What about you? What do you do for a living?
那你呢?你在哪兒高就?

A I work as an assistant in a law firm.
我在一家律師事務所當助理。

B I bet you know a lot of secret files.
我敢說你知道很多祕密檔案。

 track 013

A 常說的話

Are you a student or are you working at the moment?
你現在是學生還是在工作?

What do you major in in the university?
你在大學主修什麼?

Why do you major in this subject?
為什麼你要主修這個科目?

Is Chinese Studies popular among American college students?
美國大學生喜歡主修漢學嗎?

What do you do for a living?
你從事何行業?

Are you here in Taiwan for business or for leisure?
你來台灣是為了洽商或度假?

Make the most out of your trip in Taiwan this time.
你更要好好把握你這次在台灣的假期。

If I were a student like you, I would backpack in a foreign country like you.
要是我跟你一樣是個學生,我也會當背包客到國外旅遊。

❷常說的話

May I ask what kind of work you do?
冒昧請問一下,你是從事哪類的工作?

Is your work in the trading company very tiring?
你在貿易公司的工作很累嗎?

How long have you been working in this company?
你在這家公司工作了多久?

Are your boss and colleagues kind to you?
你的老闆和同事對你好嗎?

Do you have to work overtime very often?
你經常需要加班嗎?

Do you get extra pay for your overtime work?
你加班有加班費嗎?

Do you get a lot of holidays in a year?
你一年放很多假嗎?

Would you go abroad for working holidays?
你會為打工度假出國嗎?

Unit 7

Let me show you around in Taiwan.
讓我帶你遊台灣。

● 情境對話 1

A I can show you around if you like.
要是你喜歡的話,我可以帶你遊台灣。

B Yes, thank you. That's very kind of you.
好啊,謝謝。你人真好。

A What would you like to see first?
首先你想看什麼?

B If you don't mind, I'd like to sit down in a park now.
如果你不介意的話,現在我想要找個公園坐坐。

A 228 Park is a ten-minute walk from where we are.
二二八公園離我們這兒只有十分鐘路程。

B I'm glad there is a park right near the train station.
真高興有個公園離火車站這麼近。

014 track 跨頁共同導讀

情境對話2

A Do you have any special places you'd like to visit?
你有特別想要去的地方嗎?

B Not really. I haven't read any guidebooks yet.
沒有,我還沒讀任何導遊書籍。

A In that case, I can be your tour guide if that suits you.
要是這樣的話,如果你接受,我可以當你的導遊。

B Thank you so much. I'll follow you wherever you go.
真多謝你了。你到哪裡去,我就會跟到哪裡。

A I am thinking of going to the Xinyi Shopping District.
我想到信義商圈去。

B That sounds just fine because I am starving.
聽起來挺不錯的,因為我快餓扁了。

A You'll find many different kinds of restaurants over there.
在那兒你可以看到各式各樣的餐廳。

B After the meal, I'd like to take a look at the products there.
吃飽後我要好好看一下那邊的商品。

Chapter 2

Tourist Spots in Taipei
台北觀光景點

Unit 1 National Palace Museum
國立故宮博物院

Visiting the National Palace Museum is a must if you come to Taiwan.
來到台灣一定要去國立故宮博物院參觀。

情境對話 1

A We are about to begin a tour of Chinese art at the National Palace Museum.
現在我們就要開始國立故宮博物院的中國藝術之旅。

B This place looks to me truly like a palace.
這個地方看起來還真的像個宮殿。

A What kind of Chinese art is your favorite?
你最喜歡那類中國藝術？

B Personally, I like Chinese painting the best.
我個人最喜歡中國國畫。

A Today they happen to have an exhibition of Chinese painting.
今天他們剛好有個中國國畫展。

B Why don't we join the tour led by this English curator?
那我們何不加入這個英語解說員的導覽？

track 跨頁共同導讀 016

情境對話 2

A We are now at the National Palace Museum, a paradise for art lovers.
我們正位於國立故宮博物院,一個藝術愛好者的樂園。

B The architecture of this place does appear to me like a paradise.
這地方的建築真的看起來像個樂園。

A The museum houses more precious works of Chinese art than any other places in the world.
這博物館收藏有世界上最多的珍貴中國藝術品。

B No wonder so many visitors flock into this museum each day.
難怪每天有這麼多訪客成群湧入這個博物館。

A The themes of the exhibitions here are very interesting.
這兒展覽的主題都很有意思。

B It is said that their special exhibitions change very often.
聽說這兒的特展經常變更。

A Besides, many scholars are often invited to give speeches here.
除此之外,很多學者經常受邀來此演講。

B We'd better head for the exhibition room now.
現在我們該快點到展覽室去。

④常說的話

The National Palace Museum is surrounded by beautiful scenery.
國立故宮博物院為美景所環繞。

The National Palace Museum is one of the best museums in the world.
國立故宮博物院是世界上數一數二的博物館。

There are two types of exhibitions here, permanent and special exhibitions.
展覽分為常設展和特展兩類。

Special exhibitions often attract the most attention.
特展通常吸引了最多的目光。

Calligraphy is much appreciated in Taiwan.
在台灣很多人懂得欣賞書法。

One of the most famous artifacts in the museum is the Jade Cabbage.
翠玉白菜是館內最出名的藝術文物之一。

Unit 2

National Chiang Kai-shek Memorial Hall
國立中正紀念堂

National Chiang Kai-shek Memorial Hall is impressive.
國立中正紀念堂令人印象深刻。

情境對話 1

A Do you see that huge white building with the blue roof?
你看到那棟藍色屋頂的大型白色建築物嗎？

B Is that the famous National Chiang Kai-shek Memorial Hall?
那就是有名的國立中正紀念堂嗎？

A Correct. The architecture of the building is very Chinese.
沒錯。那建築非常中式。

B So are the styles of the gardens and walls of the park.
花園和公園圍牆的風格也是。

A Quite a few interesting exhibitions are held here.
許多有意思的展覽也於此舉行。

B Let's go in and check it out.
我們快進去看看。

情境對話2

A Do you feel like visiting the National Chiang Kai-shek Memorial Hall?
你想要參觀國立中正紀念堂嗎？

B Of course, I never had the chance to do so.
當然好，我還沒有機會進去過。

A The white building and blue tiles plus red flowers are the colors of our national flag.
白色建築、藍瓦和紅花，這些顏色是我們國旗的顏色。

B I like the arched doors here in particular.
我特別喜歡這兒的拱門。

A Many special exhibitions are held in the main hall.
大廳會舉辦很多特展。

B What sorts of special exhibitions can visitors see here?
訪客能在這兒看到什麼樣的特展呢？

A Anything you can think of, including historical documents and photos, art, dinosaurs, etc.
任何你想得到的，包括歷史文獻和照片，藝術、恐龍等。

track 跨頁共同導讀 018

B This memorial hall is quite multi-functional.
這紀念堂有多樣性功能。

---

track 019
A 常說的話

The surrounding park is spacious and well-maintained.
周圍的公園很大,而且維護得很好。

This place attracts many young people who are into street dancing.
這個地方吸引了很多喜愛街舞的年輕人。

The color of blue and white of the architecture symbolizes the national emblem.
建築物上的藍色和白色象徵國徽。

The 89 steps in the two stairs mean the 89 years of the late president.
兩排台階共有 89 階梯,代表先總統 89 年壽命。

The library here is ideal for people doing research.
對於從事研究的人來說,這兒的圖書館非常理想。

Visitors can buy souvenirs related to the late president here.
訪客在這裡可以買到先總統的相關紀念品。

019 track 跨頁共同導讀

Together with the National Theater and Concert Hall, the National Chiang Kai-shek Memorial Hall looks magnificent.
國立中正紀念堂加上國家戲劇院及音樂廳,看來富麗堂皇。

Sometimes there are social events held in the Liberty Square.
在自由廣場有時候會舉行社會活動。

B常說的話

Inside of the tall main hall, what can visitors see?
訪客能夠在高大的大廳內看見些什麼?

When was the Chiang Kai-shek Memorial Hall built?
國立中正紀念堂建於何時?

Did the late president, Mr. Chiang Kai-shek, work here?
先總統蔣介石先生曾於此處工作過嗎?

Do they have the changing of the guards here?
這兒有衛兵交接儀式嗎?

track 跨頁共同導讀 019

These walls are designed in a traditional Chinese style.
這些圍牆是以傳統中國風格設計的。

Where did "the Liberty Square" get its name?
「自由廣場」是依什麼而命名的?

What are the two palace-like buildings nearby for?
旁邊的兩棟宮殿式建築的用途為何?

Would you like to take a walk with me in the park?
你想和我一起在公園散個步嗎?

Unit 3

National Theater and Concert Hall
國家戲劇院和音樂廳

The National Theater and Concert Hall are ideal for watching performances.
國家戲劇院和音樂廳是觀看表演的理想場所。

情境對話 1

A There will soon be this performance of Russian Ballet in the National Theater.
俄國芭蕾近日將於國家戲劇院演出。

B Are the dancers really from Russia?
那些舞者真的是來自俄國嗎？

A Yes, and the tickets are about to be sold out.
對，票快要賣光了。

B The prices of the tickets must be very high, right?
票價一定很高，對吧？

A No, not really, and there is special discount for students.
不會很高。而且學生有特別優惠。

B Then I'll join you.
那麼我也要和你去看。

情境對話 2

A Didn't you say you'd like to see the Chinese instruments?
你不是說你想看看中國的樂器嗎?

B It would be even better if I could listen to Chinese music.
要是能夠聽聽中國的音樂會更好。

A If you're free this Saturday evening, I'd like to treat you to a concert in the National Concert Hall.
你這週六晚上若有空,我想請你到國家音樂廳聽音樂會。

B That's very generous of you.
你真慷慨。

A It is a concert performed by the Taipei Chinese Orchestra.
那場音樂會是由台北市立國樂團表演的。

B People say the National Concert Hall looks like a palace.
聽說國家音樂廳看起來像宮殿。

A Besides, the National Concert Hall is designed well for sound effects.
除此之外,國家音樂廳的音效設計非常好。

020 track 跨頁共同導讀

B On Saturday I'll bring my camera with me for sure.
星期六我一定會帶我的相機去。

021 track

Ⓐ常說的話

The National Theater and Concert Hall are open to Taiwanese and international performers.
國家戲劇院和音樂廳提供表演空間給台灣和國際性的表演者。

The Recital Hall and Experimental Theater are designed for smaller performances.
演奏廳和實驗劇場是為了較小型的表演而設計的。

Many Taiwanese performance groups became famous after performing in the National Theater and Concert Hall.
很多台灣的表演團體是先在國家戲劇院和音樂廳表演後才出名。

They provide the art enthusiasts with their calendar of cultural events.
他們提供文化祭節目表給藝術愛好者。

track 跨頁共同導讀 021

The service of online ticket booking saves many people much precious time.
線上訂票服務省下很多人許多寶貴時間。

Over there, famous artists are often invited to give speeches to the public.
很多知名的藝術家經常受邀在那兒對大眾演講。

Sometimes a public broadcasting of some performances will be shown at the same time in the square.
有時候某些表演會同步於廣場播放給大眾看。

Ⓑ常說的話●

How much does a student ticket for a concert cost?
一場音樂會的學生票要多少錢?

I wonder what it would feel like to listen to music in such a great place.
不知道在這麼棒的地方聽音樂是什麼感覺。

The foreign performance groups invited to perform here must be really excellent.
受邀來這裡演出的外國表演團體一定非常優秀。

What sorts of concerts are given in the Recital Hall?
什麼樣的音樂會在演奏廳表演?

021 **track** 跨頁共同導讀

The collection of performances here is really wide.
這裡的表演真可說是包羅萬象。

My Chinese teacher told me to come here to watch Chinese Opera.
我的中文老師要我來這裡來看京劇。

I'd like to watch performances, which are typical Chinese or Taiwanese.
我想要看看有代表性的中國或台灣的表演。

These two splendid structures with the golden roof are really unique.
這兩個有金色屋頂的輝煌建築物真是非常獨特。

track 022

Unit 4 Sun Yat-sen Memorial Hall
國父紀念館

Both tourists and locals like to go to the Sun Yat-sen Memorial Hall.
觀光客和當地人都愛去國父紀念館。

●情境對話 1

A Let me take you to the Sun Yat-sen Memorial Hall.
我帶你去國父紀念館。

B Was it built in memory of your National Father?
那是為了紀念你們國父所建的嗎？

A I'm very surprised at your knowledge of Asian history.
你對於亞洲歷史的了解真令我驚訝。

B Please tell me more about Dr. Sun Yat-sen later.
等一下請多告訴我孫中山先生的故事。

A Just follow me to the exhibition room inside when we are there.
我們到了那兒，請跟我去展覽室。

B I am happy to learn about his life story.
我很高興能多知道他的生平故事。

情境對話 2

A How do you like the Sun Yat-sen Memorial Hall?
你喜歡國父紀念館的建築嗎？

B I like its elegant golden roof.
我喜歡那優雅的金色屋頂。

A This place was built to commemorate our nation's Founding Father, Dr. Sun Yat-sen.
這地方是為了紀念我們國父孫中山先生所建的。

B What can we see inside of this magnificent building?
這莊嚴的建築物內有些什麼可參觀的？

A In the main hall, we can see a huge statue of Dr. Sun Yat-sen and the changing of the guards.
正廳可以看到孫中山先生大型的雕像和衛兵交接儀式。

B What are the other rooms for?
其它的房間是用來作什麼的呢？

跟老外介紹台灣這本全包了

track 跨頁共同導讀 022

Ⓐ The library, exhibition rooms and the hall for performances are open to the public.
圖書館、展覽室和表演廳都對大眾開放。

Ⓑ I can see this Memorial Hall provides all people with different services.
可見這紀念館能提供所有人各種不同的服務。

track 023

Ⓐ 常說的話

How do you like the architectural style of the Sun Yat-sen Memorial Hall?
你喜歡國父紀念館的建築風格嗎?

The park around the Sun Yat-sen Momorial Hall is very well maintained.
國父紀念館周圍的公園維護得很好。

I used to play around the fountains very often when I was a kid.
我小時候經常在噴水池邊玩耍。

In the evening, there is a special water display in the fountains.
傍晚時噴水池有特別的噴水表演。

From this point, you can see the Taipei 101 standing over there.
在這裡你可以看到台北 101 聳立在那兒。

I often come to the park around the Sun Yat-sen Memorial Hall to relax.
我時常到國父紀念館周圍的公園來放鬆。

Many art exhibitions there are free, and the quality is good.
那裡的很多展覽都是免費的,而且十分優質。

Ⓑ常說的話

The architect of the Sun Yat-sen Memorial Hall did a very good job.
設計國父紀念館的建築師可說是非常成功。

The Sun Yat-sen Memorial Hall gives people a peaceful atmosphere.
國父紀念館帶給人們祥和之氣。

Do you often watch performances in the spacious hall?
你常常到大廳觀賞表演嗎?

How many seats are there in the performance hall?
在表演廳內有多少座位?

If there is an exhibition of Chinese brush painting there, please let me know.
要是有中國水墨畫展,請通知我一下。

I am sure in the morning there would be many people doing Tai Chi in the park.
我想早上一定會有一大群人在公園打太極拳。

I see many old and young people flying kites in the park.
我看到很多人,不分年紀大小,在公園放風箏。

I wouldn't mind living next to the Sun Yat-sen Memorial Hall.
住在國父紀念館附近對我而言是挺不錯的。

Unit 5: Taipei 101
台北101

You wouldn't want to miss the firework show of Taipei 101.
你絕對不可錯過台北101的煙火秀。

●情境對話1●

A I'll take you to see the new landmark of Taipei, Taipei 101.
我要帶你去看台北101,台北的一個新地標。

B I wonder why it is called "Taipei 101".
我很好奇這棟樓為何叫「台北101」。

A "100 plus 1" means the beginning of a new century.
一百加上一,代表一個新世紀的開始。

B That sounds like a fresh new start.
聽起來像是個全新的開始。

A For that reason, there are 101 floors in this tall building.
因此這棟高樓有101層樓。

B That is really a very creative idea.
這真有創意。

情境對話 2

A Do you see the tall building over there? That is the famous Taipei 101.
你看到那邊的那棟高樓嗎？那就是著名的台北101。

B Where does the building get its name, "Taipei 101"?
那棟大樓為何叫「台北101」？

A It's a 101-storey tall skyscraper.
這棟摩天大樓有101層樓。

B Are there special meanings in the design of the tall building?
這棟高樓的設計有什麼特殊意義嗎？

A It looks like bamboo, which means success in the Chinese culture.
這建築物看起來像竹子，而竹子在中國文化中代表成功。

B I heard that the elevator in the building is the fastest in the world.
我聽說這棟樓的電梯世界第一快速。

A Every day, many visitors take the elevator to the observatory to view Taipei from above.
每天都有許多遊客搭乘這電梯到觀景台俯瞰台北。

B That's exactly what I'd like to do right now. Let's go!
我現在就想這麼做（俯瞰台北）。我們走吧！

Ⓐ 常說的話

101 means going one better than 100, the best score here.
101 意思是比 100 還要更進一步，100 是這裡最高的分數。

Visitors can go to an indoor viewing area to view Taipei on the 89th floor.
訪客能到 89 樓室內觀景台俯瞰台北。

This tall tower with eight segments looks like an Asian pagoda.
這座八層的高塔看起來像亞洲的寶塔。

Many high-class restaurants and boutiques occupy several floors of Taipei 101.
台北 101 內有好幾樓都是高檔的餐廳和精品店。

With lighting in the evening, Taipei 101 looks even more attractive than usual.
台北 101 傍晚的燈光秀使這棟高樓看來比平常更吸引人。

跟老外介紹台灣這本全包了

track 跨頁共同導讀 025

The lighting for each day in a week is different from each other.
每星期的每一天都和其它天的燈光秀不一樣。

You wouldn't want to miss the firework show of Taipei 101 at the New Year's Eve.
你絕對不可錯過除夕夜的台北 101 煙火秀。

Ⓑ常說的話

I can't believe I am going to visit the world-famous Taipei 101.
我真不敢相信我即將要去參觀舉世聞名的台北 101。

Is Taipei 101 still the tallest building in the world now?
台北 101 現在仍是世界上最高的建築物嗎？

Can we go to the top of Taipei 101?
我們能到台北 101 的頂樓嗎？

The view from the top of Taipei 101 must be very fantastic.
台北 101 頂樓的景觀一定非常精彩。

Do you like the design of this skyscraper?
你喜歡這棟摩天大樓的設計嗎？

025 track 跨頁共同導讀

Are there special meanings in the design of this building?
這棟建築物的設計有什麼特別意義嗎?

The architect is very creative in his design of this modern building.
設計這棟現代建築物的建築師非常有創意。

Did it cost a lot of money to build such a tall skyscraper?
建這樣高的摩天大樓花了一筆很大的經費嗎?

Unit 6 National Historical Museum
國立歷史博物館

track 026

You will love the National Historical Museum.
你會喜歡國立歷史博物館。

●情境對話 1●

A Right in front of you is the National Historical Museum.
在你眼前的就是國立歷史博物館。

B The ancient Chinese style of this building looks very nice.
這古中國的建築風格看起來很不錯。

A Exhibitions are held on each of the four floors.
四層樓中每一層都有展覽展出。

B The staff here is very friendly to all visitors.
工作人員對參觀者都非常友善。

A Now you will have to decide which exhibition we will start with.
現在你得決定我們要從哪一個展覽開始看了。

B What about the Buddhist sculptures?
佛教雕刻如何?

● 情境對話2 ●

A You will love the National Historical Museum with the surrounding lotus pond.
你會喜歡周圍有荷花池的國立歷史博物館。

B It's such an elegant architecture with style.
這棟優雅的建築物很有格調。

A Throughout the year, various exhibitions are shown on the four floors.
一整年當中都有不同的展覽於四層樓內展出。

B Do they have exhibitions of historical objects most of the time?
大部份時間都是歷史文物的展覽嗎？

A Most of the time, but not always. Last time they held an exhibition of "Pop-up books" there.
大部份時間是的，但並非全是。上次那兒辦了個「立體書」的展覽。

B I am sure many parents took their kids to see it.
想必很多家長有帶他們小孩去看。

A From the second floor, you can look down at the entire lotus pond.
從二樓看下去，你可以看到整個荷花池。

B What a feast to the eyes!
真是視覺的饗宴！

Ⓐ 常說的話

Art lovers cannot miss the National Historical Museum in Taipei.
藝術愛好者不能錯過台北的國立歷史博物館。

All exhibitions are carefully planned by the specialists here.
這裡的展覽都是由專業人員細心規劃的。

Their exhibition of the Tibetan Buddhist art in 2012 was very successful.
他們 2012 年的藏傳佛教藝術展非常成功。

Many schools organize school outings to visit the National Historical Museum.
很多學校安排校外教學到國立歷史博物館參觀。

The books published by the National Historical Museum have a good reputation.
國立歷史博物館所出版的書頗負聲譽。

Usually it is not very crowded in this museum.
這個博物館通常不會很擠。

On the second floor, you can watch the beautiful lotuses over coffee.
在二樓你可以一邊喝咖啡一邊觀賞美麗的荷花。

Many people like to take a walk in the Taipei Botanic Garden nearby.
很多人喜歡到附近的台北植物園散步。

027 常說的話

Could you please explain to me the meaning of this calligraphy?
你能夠為我解釋一下這書法內容的意義嗎?

Have you learned to do Chinese brush painting?
你學過中國水墨畫嗎?

I truly admire the spirit of the volunteers here.
我真欽佩這裡的志工的精神。

Taiwanese art is seldom seen outside of Taiwan.
在台灣以外的地方很少有機會看到台灣藝術。

Have you seen any exhibitions of contemporary Taiwanese art here?
你在這兒看到過當代台灣藝術的展覽嗎?

Do they have English publications for someone like me?
他們有提供英文出版物給像我這樣的人嗎?

What a shame that I missed the exhibition of "Pop-up books"!
我錯過了「立體書」的展覽,真是太可惜了!

The National Historical Museum has brought art closer to the public.
國立歷史博物館將大眾和藝術的距離拉近。

Unit 7 Beitou
北投

You should go to Beitou to bathe in the hot springs.
你一定要去北投泡湯。

情境對話 1

A Have you bathed in hot springs before?
你以前泡過湯嗎?

B No, thank you for taking me here.
沒有,謝謝你帶我來。

A How are you feeling in the hot pool now?
你現在在熱池感覺如何?

B I feel a bit light-headed.
我覺得有點頭暈。

A How about cooling down in the cold pool?
要不要到冷池涼快一下?

B That sounds good. I'll change to the cold pool in a minute.
聽起來不錯。等一下我就會改到冷池泡一泡。

track 跨頁共同導讀 028

●情境對話 2●

A Would you like to go to Beitou to bathe in the hot springs with me?
你要和我一起去北投泡湯嗎？

B That's a good idea. Should I wear a bathing suit over there?
這主意聽來不錯。在那兒我得要穿泳衣嗎？

A Yes, because we are going to bathe in the outdoor public bathing pools in Beitou.
要，因為我們要去北投戶外大眾池泡湯。

B With so many hot and cold pools, which one should I begin with?
有這麼多熱池和冷池，我該先從哪一池開始？

A Many people enjoy switching from the hot pool to the cold one and back and forth.
很多人喜歡從熱池換到冷池，來回換著泡。

B This water seems to be very unique, and its smell is very strong.
這水似乎非常特殊，而且氣味很強烈。

A It contains sulfur and has healing effects.
它含有硫磺，具有療效。

B The scenery nearby is very refreshing.
周圍的風景很能提振精神。

跟老外介紹台灣這本全包了

track 029

Ⓐ 常說的話

Have you bathed in an outdoor public bathing pool in Taiwan before?
在台灣你曾經於戶外大眾池泡過湯嗎？

If you come to Taiwan, you must try bathing in hot springs.
如果你來到台灣，一定要試試泡湯。

All the people bathing in the outdoor public bathing pool in Beitou have to wear bathing suits.
所有在北投戶外大眾池泡湯的人都必須要穿泳衣。

Before dipping into the outdoor public bathing pool, you have to wash your body first.
你得要先把身體洗乾淨，才能到戶外大眾池泡湯。

You cannot take towels with you into the public bathing pools in order to keep the water clean.
不可以將毛巾帶入大眾池泡湯，這樣才能保持水質乾淨。

You'll feel very relaxed and sleep very well tonight after bathing in the public bathing pools here.
在這裡的大眾池泡完湯後，今晚你會感到很放鬆且睡得很好。

track 跨頁共同導讀 029

If you feel like it, I can show you the Beitou Hot Springs Museum nearby.
如果你有興趣，我可以帶你去旁邊的北投溫泉博物館參觀。

B 常說的話

Do males and females bathe in the same public bathing pool in Beitou?
在北投大眾池，男生和女生是一起泡湯的嗎？

Should I take a dip in the hot pool or the cold one first?
我該先到熱池或冷池泡湯？

Could I sit on the edge of the pool and bathe my feet only?
我可以坐在池邊，只泡我的腳嗎？

The water has a very unique smell. What does it contain?
這水有個特殊氣味，它含有什麼成分？

The price of the entry ticket is really very low.
這入場券的價格實在非常低。

After bathing in the hot springs, I feel my skin is already smoother than before.
泡完湯後，我感到我的皮膚已經比以前光滑了。

If I live nearby, I'll come to the hot springs in Beitou every day.
要是我住在這附近,我會每天來北投泡湯。

Thank you for this nice experience of bathing in the hot springs.
謝謝你帶我來這裡來體驗泡湯。

Unit 8 Maokong 貓空

track 030

A trip to Maokong is refreshing for those living in a city.
對住在城市的人來說,去一趟貓空能提振精神。

●情境對話1●

A Would you like to go to Maokong with me?
你想要和我一起去貓空嗎?

B What is special about that place?
在那兒有些什麼特別的呢?

A Over there they have the closest tea farms to Taipei.
那兒有離台北最近的茶園。

B I can expect some good tea there.
在那兒我一定能有好茶喝。

A Of course, there are also many good restaurants with tea dishes.
當然,那兒還有不少很好的茶食餐廳。

B Tea dishes? I can't wait to taste them!
茶食?我等不及要嚐嚐看!

● 情境對話2 ●

A I'll take you to Maokong by gondola.
我可以帶你搭纜車去貓空。

B Can I have the view of the entire Taipei on the gondola?
我能從纜車俯瞰整個台北嗎?

A Sure you can because you'll be taken up in the middle of mountains.
當然可以,因為你會往上搭乘到山群中。

B I can't wait to experience it.
我等不及要試試看。

A Once we get there, you can pick any tea restaurant you like.
我們一到那兒,你就能挑一家你喜歡的茶食餐廳。

B Why are they called "tea restaurants"?
為何叫「茶食餐廳」呢?

A They sell not only tea but also excellent dishes cooked with tea.
那兒不但賣茶,同時也賣含茶的美食。

B That's something I have never tasted before.
那是我從來沒嚐過的。

Ⓐ 常說的話

On the gondola to Maokong, you can have a bird's-eye view of Taipei.
在到貓空的纜車上,你可以鳥瞰台北。

Maokong is the first leisure tea farm in Taiwan.
貓空是台灣第一個休閒茶園。

The heights of the hills in Maokong are suitable for growing tea.
貓空坡地的高度適合種茶。

It's very relaxing to walk through the tea farms in Maokong.
散步於貓空的茶園非常能紓壓。

Ⓑ 常說的話

How long does the gondola to Maokong take?
到貓空的纜車要花多久的時間?

What is this special Crystal Cabin like?
水晶車廂有什麼特別的地方?

Are there trekking paths in Maokong?
在貓空有健行步道嗎?

I'd like to experience picking tea in Maokong.
我想在貓空體驗一下採茶。

Chapter 3

Northern Scenic Spots
北部風景區

Unit 1　Keelung
基隆

Keelung is well-known for its night market delicacies.
基隆以夜市美食聞名。

情境對話 1

A Can you smell the sea air?
你聞到了空中海水的味道嗎？

B Yes, I guess we have arrived at Keelung.
聞到了，我猜我們已經到基隆了。

A It used to be the largest port in Taiwan.
基隆曾經是台灣第一大港。

B There must be great seafood in this place.
這裡一定有很棒的海鮮。

A Let's go to Keelung Bisha Fishing Port for some fresh seafood.
我們一起去基隆碧砂漁港吃點新鮮海鮮。

B My mouth is watering now.
我已經在流口水了。

track 跨頁共同導讀 032

情境對話 2

A Keelung Miaokou Night Market attracts thousands of visitors.
基隆廟口夜市吸引了無數觀光客。

B What does "Miaokou" mean?
「廟口」是什麼意思？

A "Maokou" means the entrance of a temple, where the night market began.
「廟口」是廟的入口，夜市開始形成的地方。

B That sounds similar to the marketplaces in some cities.
聽起來，基隆廟口類似於某些城市的市集。

A Many signs of the stalls are written in Chinese, English and Japanese.
很多攤販有中文、英文和日文的招牌。

B That's very thoughtful of them.
他們設想真周到。

A Most of them sell either seafood or Keelung delicacies.
大部分店家賣海鮮美食或基隆特有小吃。

B Let's join this line waiting for Taiwanese Tempura.
我們快來排買天婦羅的隊伍吧。

Ⓐ常說的話

The Keelung fish market provides the "freshest possible" seafood.
基隆魚市提供最新鮮的海鮮。

Tourists can go on a cruise excursion with others.
旅客可以和其他人一起搭觀光遊艇。

Let's stroll on the wooden platform of Keelung Maritime Plaza.
我們去基隆海洋廣場的木棧平台上一起散步吧。

Customers can pick fish alive to let the chefs prepare them here.
客人在這裡可以挑選活魚讓主廚烹煮。

Keelung is indeed a paradise for seafood gourmets.
基隆真的是海鮮老饕的樂園。

Let me show you a restaurant with a nice view of the harbor.
我帶你去一家能看到港灣美景的餐廳。

Keelung Night Market originally started near the entrance of a temple.
基隆夜市最早是在廟的入口附近開始的。

Hoping Island features awesome rock formations.
和平島以壯麗的岩石景觀而著名。

track 跨頁共同導讀 033

B 常說的話

This is such a low price for such a fresh crab!
這樣新鮮的螃蟹真的是太便宜了！

You can't find the quality and quantity of the seafood anywhere else.
在任何別的地方你找不到這樣質和量的海鮮。

You can smell the sea air wherever you go in Keelung.
無論你到基隆哪裡，都會聞到空氣中海水的味道。

This place reminds me of Seattle, my hometown with a seaport.
這個地方讓我想到西雅圖，我的海港家鄉。

Keelung Miaokou Night Market has a special charm.
基隆廟口夜市有一種特殊的魅力。

Many stall owners offer customers a bite to taste their foods.
很多攤販生意人讓客人試吃他們的美食。

Taking a walk on the Keelung Maritime Plaza with you is refreshing.
和你在基隆海洋廣場上散步讓我感到心曠神怡。

You are very lucky to live so close to Keelung.
你住得離基隆這麼近，真是幸運。

Unit 2 Jiufen 九份

Jiufen used to be the center of gold mining in Taiwan.
九份是昔日台灣的採金礦中心。

情境對話 1

A Would you be interested in an old town of gold mining?
你會對舊日的採金礦中心感興趣嗎?

B That sounds fascinating to me.
聽起來很有意思。

A Jiufen is next to mountains, facing the sea.
九份背山面海。

B The view there must be very worth seeing.
那兒的風景一定很值得一看。

A We have to climb up the hills to see the nice views.
我們得要爬上坡才能看見美景。

B For nice views, I don't mind exercising a bit.
為了看美景,運動一下子沒關係。

track 跨頁共同導讀 034

情境對話 2

A Have you been to the old center of gold mining in Taiwan, Jiufen?
你是否到過九份,這個台灣昔日的採金礦中心?

B No, but I'd like to if you could take me there.
沒有,但是如果你能帶我,我會很樂意去。

A Surrounded by mountains, people can look out at the sea in Jiufen.
九份周圍為群山環繞,還能從那兒看到海。

B No wonder so many tea houses in Jiufen claim to have the best ocean view.
難怪這麼多九份的茶館宣稱有最佳的海景。

A Taro dish in Jiufen is the local specialty almost everyone likes.
九份的當地名產芋圓,幾乎每個人都喜歡。

B I'm sure that includes me.
我想我一定也會喜歡的。

A The Jiufen Gold Mine Museum is where you'd like to visit.
九份金礦博物館是你會想參觀的。

B You certainly know me very well.
你真的很了解我。

❶常說的話

Have you been on a one-day tour of Jiufen, the tourist town?
你到過九份這個觀光小鎮一日遊嗎?

The unique landscape of Jiufen attracts many visitors.
九份獨特的風景吸引了很多觀光客。

Quite a few well-known movies were shot in Jiufen.
很多著名的電影是在九份拍攝的。

Sweet taro balls, rice cake and meatball are popular dishes in Jiufen.
甜芋圓、米糕和肉圓是九份非常受歡迎的小吃。

In the Jiufen Gold Mine Museum, you can experience the life of a miner in the old days.
在九份金礦博物館可以體驗昔日礦工的生活。

The mining industry went down and finally ended in the 1970's.
採礦業漸漸沒落,最後於 1970 年代結束。

Both tourists and locals enjoy watching the sea at a tea house.
觀光客和當地人都喜歡坐在茶館看海。

If you want to visit the whole of Jiufen, make sure you have good sneakers on.
如果你想走遍九份,一定要穿雙好球鞋。

track 跨頁共同導讀 035

Ⓑ常說的話

I didn't know there was this old town of gold mining in northern Taiwan.
我還不知道台灣北部有這麼個昔日採金礦小鎮。

Today I learned quite a lot in the Jiufen Gold Mine Museum.
今天我在九份金礦博物館學到了很多。

Did the gold miners really have such a tough life back then?
那些昔日礦工的日子真的那麼苦嗎?

Some tea houses are situated at incredible spots.
有些茶館的地點真不錯。

Why are these paths so narrow and steep?
為何這些路徑這麼窄又這麼陡。

Why did they pick Jiufen to shoot the movies?
為什麼那些電影會挑在九份拍攝呢?

I didn't know I would have to climb so many stairs in Jiufen.
我還不知道在九份得要爬這麼多階梯。

The breath-taking scenery in Jiufen lives up to its reputation.
九份的驚人美景真是實至名歸。

Unit 3　Wulai 烏來

036 track

Wulai is famous for the hot springs and aboriginal culture.
烏來以溫泉和原住民文化而聞名。

● 情境對話 1 ●

A Do you want to go to see cherry blossoms in Wulai?
你想要到烏來賞櫻嗎？

B I didn't know there were cherry blossoms in Wulai.
我還不知道在烏來可以賞櫻。

A Wulai is also famous for its magnificent waterfalls.
烏來同時也以壯觀的瀑布而聞名。

B What else can we see in Wulai?
在烏來還有什麼可看的？

A Aboriginal culture is also featured in Wulai.
原住民文化同時也是烏來的特色。

B That sounds like my cup of tea.
聽起來我會很喜歡。

情境對話 2

A Would you like to go to Wulai to learn more about the aboriginal culture?
你想要去烏來了解更多原住民文化嗎？

B I didn't know there was any aboriginal culture in Wulai.
我還不知道原來在烏來有原住民文化。

A One whole street is dedicated to aboriginal handicraft.
有一整條街都在賣原住民手工藝品。

B I've always wanted to see things like that.
我一直很想看那些事物。

A If you are so fascinated by aboriginal culture, you should visit the Wulai Atayal Museum.
如果你對原住民文化那麼著迷，你該去烏來泰雅民族博物館。

B Is the Atayal tribe the indigenous people living in the area?
泰雅族是住在那個地區的原住民嗎？

A Yes, "Wulai" comes from the Atayal language, meaning hot spring.
對，「烏來」出自泰雅語，意思是溫泉。

B I wouldn't mind enjoying hot springs in an aboriginal town.
在原住民鎮上享受溫泉,聽起來再好不過了。

036 track 跨頁共同導讀

037 track

Ⓐ常說的話●

The Wulai hot spring water is colorless and odorless.
烏來溫泉水無色且無味。

Most visitors will stay overnight in a hot spring hotel.
大部分觀光客會在溫泉旅館過夜。

The indigenous shops on the main street sell a wide range of products.
大街上的原住民商店賣各式各樣的產品。

The Wulai Atayal Museum is special among aboriginal museums.
烏來泰雅民族博物館是很有特色的原住民博物館。

In the Wulai Gorge exist several falls, and the largest one is Wulai Falls.
在烏來峽谷中有好幾個瀑布,最大的一個是烏來瀑布。

跟老外介紹台灣這本全包了

track 跨頁共同導讀 037

Wulai Scenic Train can take tourists from downtown Wulai to the base of Wulai Falls.
烏來的觀光台車可以將旅客從烏來的市中心載到烏來瀑布的底部。

Wulai Scenic Train was built to transport lumber during the Japanese era.
烏來的觀光台車是建於日據時代用來運送木材的。

Wulai Gondola takes visitors to the top of Wulai Falls.
烏來的空中纜車將觀光客載到烏來瀑布的頂端。

B 常說的話

The cherry blossoms here certainly draw tourists from all over Taiwan.
這兒的櫻花確實是將台灣所有的觀光客吸引來了。

Such a lovely town with hot springs is bound to be a tourist destination.
這樣美麗的溫泉小鎮注定會是個觀光去處。

I particularly like the Atayal female costumes.
我特別喜愛泰雅族女性的服飾。

So many aboriginal dishes can be found along the main street!
大街上的原住民餐點非常多!

The ride on the Wulai Gondola is very smooth and comfortable.
烏來的空中纜車搭起來非常平穩且舒適。

The Wulai Gorge with waterfalls seen from the Gondola is awesome.
從空中纜車看帶有瀑布的烏來峽谷,景象非常壯觀。

Both local and foreign guests like to visit this mountainous town.
本地和外國的客人都喜歡來這山城觀光。

Unit 4 Tamsui
淡水

track 038

The closest place near Taipei to watch the sea is Tamsui.
離台北最近能看海的地方是淡水。

情境對話 1

A Where is the closest beach near Taipei?
離台北最近的海灘在哪兒?

B That would be Tamsui.
在淡水。

A Can people swim at the beach in Tamsui?
在淡水海邊能游泳嗎?

B I'm afraid not because it's not a sandy beach.
恐怕不能,因為那不是沙岸。

A What can we do over there?
那麼在那兒能做什麼?

B Why don't we go there this afternoon, and you'll find out.
我們何不下午到那兒去一趟,你就會得到答案了。

情境對話2

A Could you take me to somewhere near the sea?
你能帶我去海邊嗎?

B The closest place from here near the sea is Tamsui.
離這裡最近的海邊是淡水。

A Should I take my swimsuit with me?
我該帶我的泳衣嗎?

B That won't be necessary because swimming is not allowed there.
不需要,因為那裡不准游泳。

A I thought you said it was a beach.
你不是說那裡是海灘?

B It is a rocky coast, not like a sandy beach.
那兒是岩岸,不像沙灘。

A Why do so many people still go there?
那為何還有那麼多人去那裡?

B It's a great place to watch the sea and the people and much more.
那是個看海看人還有看很多其它事物的好地方。

跟老外介紹台灣這本全包了

track 039

Ⓐ 常說的話

Tamsui is very famous for watching the sunset at sea.
淡水以海邊看夕陽而聞名。

Many street performers like to entertain people along the sea.
很多街頭藝人喜歡在海邊娛樂大眾。

On holidays, Tamsui is usually crowded with tourists and food stands.
在假日,淡水經常擠滿觀光客和攤販。

You should try the local special dishes in Tamsui.
你該嚐嚐淡水當地小吃。

Why not take the ferry boat to Bali and check out what's over there?
何不搭乘渡輪到八里看看那兒有些什麼?

The Rainbow Bridge is one of the most popular spots in northern Taiwan.
彩虹大橋是北台灣最受歡迎的景點之一。

Taking a walk along the sea shore is very relaxing and refreshing.
在海邊散步非常能令人放鬆,很能提振精神。

039 track 跨頁共同導讀

If you're into historical sites, you wouldn't be disappointed in Tamsui.
如果你對歷史古蹟有興趣，在淡水你不會感到失望。

B 常說的話

In Tamsui, I see many restaurants with ocean view along the way.
在淡水我一路走下來，看見了很多海景餐廳。

Just eating the local small specialties makes me already full.
光吃當地小吃，我就已經感到飽了。

Watching the sunset at sea in Tamsui is something very unique.
在淡水的海邊看夕陽，是非常獨特的經驗。

I can see why so many people take their whole family here on holidays.
我可以了解為何這麼多的人在假日帶全家人來這裡。

The ride of the ferry boat is very rough yet exciting.
搭渡輪非常驚險卻刺激。

track 跨頁共同導讀 039

Many kids like to interact with the street performers.
很多小孩喜歡和街頭藝人互動。

Fort San Domingo is really very impressive and well-preserved.
紅毛城真是令人印象深刻,而且保存得很好。

The trip to Tamsui has been very educational and entertaining.
淡水之行非常寓教於樂。

Unit 5 Yingge 鶯歌

Pottery comes to my mind when I hear Yingge.
聽到鶯歌,我就想到陶器。

情境對話 1

A Have you made any pottery yourself?
你曾自己動手做過陶器嗎?

B Never. Have you?
不曾。你呢?

A Yes, and I am going to take you to Yingge to experience pottery making.
我做過,而且我要帶你去鶯歌體驗做陶器。

B Really? Do you think I can make pottery on my own?
真的?你覺得我能自己動手做陶器?

A Even kids can D.I.Y. pottery there, with a good teacher, of course.
在那裡連小孩子也會自己動手做陶器,不過當然是跟著老師學。

B If you say so, sign me up.
既然你這麼說了,幫我報名吧。

跟老外介紹台灣這本全包了

track 跨頁共同導讀 040

●情境對話 2

A We have finally arrived in the main street of Yingge.
我們總算到達了鶯歌的大街。

B Look, that sign says beginners can learn to make pottery there!
你看,那邊有個牌子寫說初學者能在那兒學做陶器。

A You can join them to learn how to make pottery with a master.
你可以加入他們,和師傅一起學做陶器。

B Can I make whatever I want to make at the workshop?
在工作坊中我可以做任何我想做的嗎?

A I think so, but have a talk with the master first.
我想可以,但是先問一下師傅吧。

B Most people seem to be busy making cups.
大部分人似乎都在忙著做杯子。

A They can take the cups they made back home.
最後他們可以把自己做的杯子帶回家。

B No wonder some are writing names on the cups now.
怪不得有人現在正在杯子上寫名字。

❹常說的話●

The Yingge Ceramics Museum is the first pottery museum in Taiwan.
鶯歌陶瓷博物館是台灣第一個陶瓷博物館。

Taiwanese pottery art is a special feature in the Yingge Ceramics Museum.
台灣的陶瓷藝術是鶯歌陶瓷博物館的一個特色。

In all the pottery artworks you've seen, which one do you like best?
在你看過的陶瓷藝術品中,你最喜歡哪一個?

Making pottery on your own is one important part of the tour in Yingge.
自己動手做陶器是鶯歌之旅重要的一部分。

Wherever you go in Yingge, pottery can be seen in almost all shops.
在鶯歌無論你到哪裡,幾乎在所有店家都可以看到陶器。

Take your time shopping in the pottery shops in this neighborhood.
慢慢逛這附近的陶器店家。

You'll have to carry the pottery in your carry-on bags for your flight.
搭飛機時,你可能得用手提袋提陶器。

track 跨頁共同導讀 042

情境對話 2

A Right in front of you is the Zushi Temple, a historic site, too.
在你面前的是祖師廟,也是個歷史古蹟。

B Is this the spectacular temple, which draws visitors to come to Sanxia?
就是吸引觀光客來到三峽的那間華麗廟宇嗎?

A You are right, and the temple worships Qingshui Master.
你說對了,這間廟祭拜清水祖師。

B The stone lions at the front gate are so full of life.
在門前的石獅看起來栩栩如生。

A They are designed by Mr. Li Meishu, who led the restoration of the temple.
石獅是李梅樹先生所設計的,廟的重建工程由他所指揮。

B The walls and columns of the Zushi Temple are all sculpted from stone.
祖師廟的牆和柱子都是用石頭所雕刻的。

A If you look closer, you'll find a wide variety of styles.
你細看的話,可以看到各式各樣的風格。

042 track 跨頁共同導讀

B They are unique, amazing and detailed works of art.
真的是特別又驚人的細緻藝術品。

043 track

常說的話

Pay close attention to the window details and you'll see the fish design.
你細看窗戶的細節的話,就會看到魚的設計圖樣。

Every column is carved with a different design.
每個柱子上面所刻的設計圖樣都不一樣。

The carvings on the walls appear to be like paintings.
牆上的雕刻像是畫上去的。

Take a close look at the ceiling of the temple.
仔細看看廟裡的天花板。

The Sanxia Zushi Temple is a good example of heritage restoration.
三峽祖師廟是古蹟重建的好例子。

The Old Street in Sanxia is full of buildings of the last century.
三峽的老街充滿了上個世紀的建築物。

track 跨頁共同導讀 043

Greek, Roman and baroque styles are found in these old houses.
在這些老屋中可以看到希臘、羅馬和巴洛克風格。

The Old Street in Sanxia is the longest preserved original old street in Taiwan.
三峽的老街是台灣保存至今最長的老街。

B 常說的話

What did the Qingshui Master do during his lifetime?
清水祖師在生前做過什麼？

Is Mr. Li Meishu himself an artist from Taiwan?
李梅樹先生本身是位台灣藝術家嗎？

What are some of the major works Mr. Li Meishu has done?
李梅樹先生重要的作品有哪些？

Mr. Li Meishu's devotion in the restoration of the temple should be appreciated.
李梅樹先生對重建祖師廟的貢獻令人感佩。

Are most temples in Taiwan facing the problems of restoration?
台灣大部分的廟宇都面臨重建的問題嗎？

I can see the columns of the temple are carved with expert skills.
我看得出來寺廟的柱子是專家的雕刻作品。

It's hard to believe that you can see such first-rate art in a small temple.
在這樣小的廟裡能見到這樣極致的藝術，真令人不敢置信。

On the Old Street, some owners' names can still be seen on the old houses.
在老街可以看到有些屋主的名字仍在古屋上。

Unit 7 Bitan Scenic Area
碧潭風景區

The natural beauty in the Bitan Scenic Area is stunning.
碧潭風景區有令人驚艷的自然美景。

情境對話 1

A Look at the peaceful Lake in the Bitan Scenic Area.
你看碧潭真寧靜。

B This suspension bridge over the lake makes it look even better.
碧潭上的吊橋使湖水看起來更美。

A The beauty of nature can be easily found here.
在這兒大自然之美到處可見。

B People on the pedal boats look so happy.
腳踏船裡的人看來真快樂。

A Would you like to walk with me on lake side?
你想和我一起在湖邊散步嗎?

B That's a good idea.
這主意不錯。

情境對話2

A We've now arrived at the Bitan Scenic Area.
我們現在到達了碧潭風景區。

B And that must be the well-known Bitan suspension bridge.
想必那就是有名的碧潭吊橋了。

A That's right. This bridge connects the two sides of the lake.
對,這橋連接起湖的兩岸。

B I see many people enjoying pedaling boats on the lake.
我看見很多人在湖中享受腳踏船的活動。

A On the lake, I can see the reflections of the sky and green mountains.
在湖面上我可以看到天空和綠山的倒影。

B Pedaling on the lake seems to be a popular leisure time activity.
在湖中踩腳踏船似乎是很受歡迎的休閒活動。

A Why don't we pick a restaurant on the lake side with a nice view?
我們何不在湖邊選一家可看美景的餐廳?

B That restaurant at the end of the bridge seems to have the best view.
位於橋尾的那家餐廳似乎有最好的景色。

跟老外介紹台灣這本全包了

track 045

Ⓐ 常說的話

The Bitan Scenic Area can be easily reached via Taipei MRT.
搭台北捷運很容易就到達碧潭風景區。

Bitan means Green Lake in Chinese.
碧潭的中文意思是綠色的湖。

On sunny days, a lot of people are on the lake, pedaling boats.
天氣晴朗時,湖中有非常多的人在踩腳踏船。

This place reminds me of my childhood experience of pedaling boats.
這地方讓我想起我童年踩腳踏船的經驗。

The cyclists love the wide cycling paths along the lake.
騎自行車的人非常喜歡湖邊寬廣的自行車車道。

The view from the suspension bridge is special and marvelous.
由吊橋看到的景色很特別,也很美麗。

Nothing relaxes you more than sitting over coffee with the view of the lake.
沒有什麼比一邊喝咖啡一邊賞湖還能令人放鬆。

045 track 跨頁共同導讀

B常說的話

Such gorgeous scenery is hard to find near the Taipei city.
這麼美的景色在台北市附近很難找到。

Now I know how easy it is to get to the Bitan Scenic Area, I'll often come here.
現在我知道來碧潭風景區這麼簡單,我會經常來這裡。

The green peaceful lake reflects the color of the mountains around it.
這碧綠又平靜的湖面反映出周圍的山色。

Without the suspension bridge, the lake would look totally different.
要是沒有了吊橋,這湖泊會看起來完全不一樣。

At such a scenic area, I enjoy doing nothing, just watching the scenery.
在這樣的風景區,我喜歡什麼都不做,只是看美景。

Next time I'll take my bike with me because of the wide cycling paths.
下次我會帶我的單車來,因為這裡的單車車道很寬。

I really appreciate you taking me to this wonderful scenic area.
我真的很感激你帶我來這個美好的風景區。

跟老外介紹台灣這本全包了

track 046

Unit 8 Daxi 大溪

People come to Daxi for the tasty dried bean curd.
人們到大溪來品嚐美味豆乾。

● 情境對話 1

A We have come to the Daxi Old Street.
我們來到了大溪老街。

B The buildings look really quite old and special.
這些建築物看來真的很古老又很特別。

A In the old days, it was the center of camphor and tea trades.
從前這裡是樟腦和茶的中心。

B What about now?
現在呢？

A Dried bean curd is the main industry in Daxi now.
豆乾是大溪現在主要的產業。

B Where can I taste the delicious dried bean curd?
我要到哪裡才能嚐到豆乾？

046 track 跨頁共同導讀

情境對話2

A Take a look at the architecture on the Daxi Old Street.
看看大溪老街的建築。

B They seem to be the mixture of eastern and western styles.
看來似乎是東方和西方風格的混合。

A They were built in Japanese baroque style during the Japanese era.
這些是建於日據時代的日式巴洛克風格的建築物。

B What are these passages designed for?
這些通道是設計來作什麼用的?

A They are built for workers to pass through as shortcuts.
他們是建來讓工人當捷徑通過。

B Those architects were so clever!
那些建築師真聰明!

A Traditional wooden furniture used to be the main industry here.
傳統的木製傢俱曾是這裡主要產業。

B No wonder they needed these passages as shortcuts.
難怪他們需要這些通道當捷徑。

跟老外介紹台灣這本全包了

track 047

Ⓐ 常說的話

When Taiwanese hear Daxi, they immediately think of dried bean curd.
台灣人一聽到大溪,都會馬上想到豆乾。

In Daxi they have all sorts of dried bean curd products you can think of.
大溪有你想得到的各式各樣豆乾產品。

No visit to Daxi is complete without tasting dried bean curd.
如果你到大溪沒有吃豆乾,就好像沒來過。

My favorite bean curd is this black one, which is seasoned in herbs for a long time.
我最喜歡的豆乾是這個黑色的,那是在香料中調味醃製了很久的豆乾。

The Daxi Street is a street full of history and cultural heritage.
大溪老街是條充滿了歷史和文化古蹟的街道。

After a short while, I'll show you the old mansions and gardens in Daxi.
等一下我會帶你看大溪的古宅和舊花園。

Walking along the Old Street takes me back to the old time.
在大溪老街散步讓我好像回到了古時候。

Each of the carvings on the roof has its special meaning.
屋頂上的每樣雕刻都有其特殊意義。

B 常說的話

Most Americans cannot imagine a town full of bean curd shops.
大部分美國人很難想像一個充滿豆乾商店的小鎮。

Back in the States, dried bean curd is not something I eat all the time.
我在美國老家不會經常吃豆乾。

All the people in Daxi seem to be in the business of dried bean curd.
似乎大溪所有的人都從事豆乾相關產業。

Since dried bean curd is good for health, I'll eat it to my heart's content.
既然豆乾對健康有益,我可要盡情地吃。

Is there a place where I can see how dried bean curd is made?
我可以到哪邊參觀豆乾的製造過程?

We are lucky to be able to see the well-maintained Daxi Old Street.
我們很幸運能見到維護得這麼好的大溪老街。

Those who lived in one of the baroque style buildings must be rich.
住在這種巴洛克建築的人一定是有錢人。

跟老外介紹台灣這本全包了

track 048

Unit 9 Jiaoxi
礁溪

Jiaoxi is a tourist town known for its hot springs.
礁溪是個以溫泉出名的觀光小鎮。

情境對話 1

A Would you like to try foot bathing in Jiaoxi?
你想要到礁溪試試泡腳嗎？

B Do you mean bathing feet in the public pool outdoors?
你是指到戶外的大眾池泡腳？

A That's right. The spring water of Jiaoxi Hot Spring is unique.
對。礁溪的溫泉水很獨特。

B Just imagine bathing feet and chatting with you at the same time...
光想到一邊泡腳一邊和你聊天…

A Don't forget the scenery around the hot spring park.
不要忘了溫泉公園附近的美景。

B All of my worries are sure to be washed away.
我所有的煩惱都會被洗淨。

048 track 跨頁共同導讀

●情境對話 2●

A You must go to Jiaoxi to try foot bathing with me.
你一定要和我去礁溪試試泡腳。

B Is that a public bathing pool only for foot bathing?
那是個專門泡腳的戶外大眾池嗎?

A Yes, unlike Beitou hot spring, in Jiaoxi there are areas only for foot bathing.
對,不同於北投溫泉,在礁溪有專門泡腳的區域。

B Is the public pool in a beautiful natural setting?
那個大眾池周圍的風景美嗎?

A The public pool is in a park, surrounded by lush trees.
那個大眾池位在公園中,周圍有青蔥的樹木。

B What are some other activities we can do there?
在那邊還有什麼其它的活動可以做?

A They offer hot spring dishes prepared with Jiaoxi hot spring water.
那兒有提供以礁溪溫泉水料理的溫泉美食。

B That is as organic as you can get.
不可能找到比這個更有機的了。

跟老外介紹台灣這本全包了

track 049

ⒶⒶ常說的話

Vegetables grown in Jiaoxi are irrigated by the hot spring water there.
在礁溪所種植的蔬菜是以那兒的溫泉水所灌溉的。

Jiaoxi hot spring has the reputation of being able to nourish skins.
礁溪溫泉有能滋潤皮膚的美名。

Before the New Year holidays, Jaoxi hot spring hotels are all fully booked.
在過年假期之前,礁溪的溫泉旅館全都被訂滿了。

The diversity of nature in Jaoxi is what Yilan County has in particular.
礁溪豐富的生態是宜蘭縣所特有的。

Ⓑ常說的話

I seem to be able to feel the healing effects of the Jiaoxi hot spring water.
我好像可以感受到礁溪溫泉水的療效。

Which hot spring hotels would you recommend to me?
你會推薦我哪家溫泉旅館?

What are some of your favorite hot spring dishes in Jiaoxi?
你最喜歡的礁溪溫泉料理是什麼?

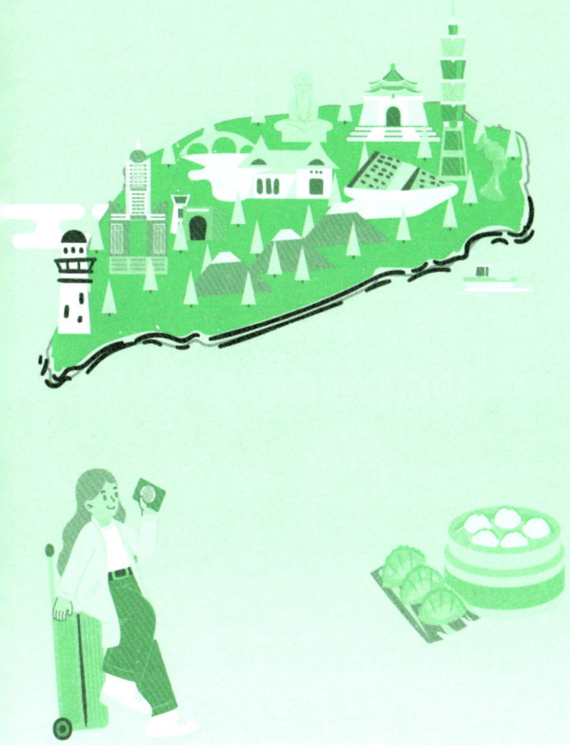

Chapter 4

Central Scenic Spots
中部風景區

Unit 1 Sanyi Township
三義鄉

Sanyi is the wood sculpture capital of Taiwan.
三義是台灣木雕藝術城。

● 情境對話 1 ●

A Sanyi is famous for its wood sculpture.
三義以木雕聞名。

B Are there many wood sculptors in this place?
在這地方有很多木雕師嗎？

A Half of the residents here live on wood sculpturing.
這裡大半的居民靠木雕為生。

B This pair of wood owl sculptures is my favorite.
這對木雕貓頭鷹是我最喜歡的。

A You'll see a lot more wood sculptures on this Street of Wood Sculpture.
在這條木雕街上，你會看見更多的木雕。

B Thank you for taking me here.
謝謝你帶我來這裡。

情境對話2

A I know you like wood sculpture, but have you sculptured one yourself?
我知道你喜歡木雕,但是你自己動手雕刻過嗎?

B Not yet. Are you saying I can DIY in the sculpture stores here?
還沒。你是說我在這些木雕店可以自己動手做嗎?

A You can also color the wood sculptures if you like.
如果你想要的話,還可以彩繪木雕。

B I'm going to make one little bird statue.
我要做個小鳥雕像。

A After that, would you like to visit the Sanyi Wood Sculpture Museum?
然後你想要參觀三義木雕博物館嗎?

B Is that a museum all about wood sculpture?
那是專門展示木雕的博物館嗎?

A That's right. It's the only museum for wood sculpture in Taiwan.
是的。那是全台灣唯一的木雕博物館。

B We must visit that museum and learn more about wood sculpture.
我們得參觀那家博物館,多學一些關於木雕的事物。

ⓐ 常說的話

The aim of the museum is to promote the art of wood sculpture.
博物館的目的是要推廣木雕藝術。

This is the only public museum in Taiwan that is for wood sculpture alone.
這是全台灣唯一專門展示木雕的公立博物館。

What kind of wood sculptures would you like to see first in the museum?
你想先看博物館內的哪一類木雕？

You can appreciate the beauty of wood furniture in this area.
在這一區你可以欣賞木製傢俱之美。

You can see they put in a lot of efforts into the preservation of wood sculpture.
你可以看出來他們盡了很大努力保存木雕。

They didn't begin the carving of religious statues in Sanyi until recently.
在三義，宗教的木雕直在最近才開始。

In order to become a wood sculpture master, one has to begin as an apprentice.
要成為木雕師傅，要從學徒開始。

This Old Street of Wood Sculpture is itself like an art gallery.
這條木雕老街本身就像藝廊。

track 跨頁共同導讀 051

B 常說的話

I would like to make my first wood sculpture here in Sanyi.
我想要在三義做我的第一個木雕。

Some shops on the Street of Wood Sculpture have DIY workshops.
這條木雕街上的某些店家有自己動手做的工作坊。

The wood bears look so real and alive.
這熊的木雕看起來好逼真、好生動。

A wood sculpture is certainly a lot easier to take home than pottery.
攜帶木雕回家要比攜帶陶器容易得多。

All kinds of subject matters in the wood sculptures can be found here.
在這兒可以找到各式各樣主題的木雕。

The style of each wood sculptor differs from another.
每位木雕師都有自己的風格。

Please show me around in the Sanyi Wood Sculpture Museum.
請帶我參觀三義木雕博物館。

What is shown in the permanent collections of the museum?
這個博物館的常設展都展些什麼?

Unit 2 Dajia Zhenlan Temple
大甲鎮瀾宮

Dajia Zhenlan Temple is the shrine for worshiping Mazu.
大甲鎮瀾宮是祭拜媽祖的殿堂。

● 情境對話 1

Ⓐ Have you heard of Mazu?
你聽過媽祖嗎？

Ⓑ Not really. Does that have to do with this temple?
沒有。和這間廟有關嗎？

Ⓐ Mazu is the goddess of sailors and fishermen.
媽祖是出海人和漁民的守護者。

Ⓑ Is this temple dedicated to her?
這間廟是用來祭拜她的嗎？

Ⓐ Yes, it is to thank Mazu for her countless sea rescues.
是的，是為了感謝媽祖無數次的海上援救。

Ⓑ I hope she will watch over my flight home, too.
希望她也能保佑我的回程。

情境對話 2

A The Dajia Zhenlan Temple is the shrine for worshiping Mazu.
大甲鎮瀾宮是祭拜媽祖的殿堂。

B Is that the goddess of the sea you mentioned to me earlier?
就是你之前對我提過的海神嗎?

A Yes, this temple becomes the center of Mazu's birthday celebration.
是的,這間廟成為媽祖誕辰慶典的中心。

B I think I once watched the parade of Mazu on Discovery Channel.
我想我曾在探索頻道看過媽祖遶境。

A Do you like the detailed columns of the Zhenlan Temple?
你喜歡鎮瀾宮細緻的廊柱嗎?

B Very much so. Is it an ancient temple?
非常喜歡。這間廟歷史很久嗎

A It was built in 1770 and was later expanded.
是在1770年所建的,後來再加以擴建。

B Many worshipers come here today even though it is not Mazu's birthday.
即使今天不是媽祖誕辰,還是有好多信眾來這兒。

Ⓐ 常說的話

Every spring, many worshipers come here for Mazu's birthday celebration.
每年春天許多信眾來這兒參加媽祖誕辰慶典。

Mazu, also spelled Matsu, is the goddess of the sea that watches over fishermen.
媽祖（也拼作 Matsu）是保佑漁民的海神。

On the Lantern Festival, a lot is drawn to decide on the exact date to start the Mazu tour.
元宵節時會抽籤決定確切哪一天開始媽祖遶境。

Worshipers travel for eight days throughout southern Taiwan.
信眾於南台灣繞境八天。

The parade of Mazu travels to sister Mazu temples in southern Taiwan.
媽祖遶境會經過南台灣其它的媽祖廟。

The Mazu tour includes Taichung, Changhua, Yunlin and Chiayi.
媽祖遶境路線包含台中、彰化、雲林和嘉義。

The total distance the worshipers travel is about 330 kilometers.
媽祖遶境路線總共約 330 公里。

The parade of Mazu is regarded as one of the major world religious festivals.
媽祖遶境為公認的世界重要宗教慶典之一。

跟老外介紹台灣這本全包了

track 跨頁共同導讀 053

Ⓑ常說的話

Dajia Zhenlan Temple is a temple with a long history of religious culture.
大甲鎮瀾宮是一間有悠久宗教文化的廟宇。

There are several incense burners in this huge temple.
在這偌大的廟宇裡有好幾個香爐。

The offerings brought by the worshipers are all over the table.
信眾帶來的供品擺滿了供桌。

That old woman seems to want me to buy her spirit money.
那位老婦人似乎想要我買她的金紙。

I like the smoky atmosphere in the temple.
我喜歡廟裡的香火味。

Next spring we should come here again to watch the Mazu tour.
明年春天我們應該再來這裡看媽祖遶境。

How can I take part in the parade of Mazu?
要怎樣才能參加媽祖遶境？

Is Mazu worshiping an important part of Taiwanese culture?
媽祖敬拜是台灣文化重要的一部分嗎？

Unit 3 Lugang
鹿港

054 track

Lugang is a historical and cultural town.
鹿港是個歷史文化小鎮。

● 情境對話 1

A How do you like the Folk Arts Museum in Lugang?
你喜歡鹿港民俗文物館嗎？

B The style of the building seems to be Victorian.
這棟建築物似乎是維多利亞風格。

A It was once the mansion of the Koo Family.
那曾是辜家的祖宅。

B No kidding.
你沒開玩笑吧。

A Let's take a look at the old life of the rich family.
我們來看看從前有錢人家的生活。

B I'm very keen to know about it.
我非常有興趣了解。

情境對話2

A Do you like the feeling of walking around Lugang?
你喜歡在鹿港四處走的感覺嗎?

B It reminds me of the old towns in some European cities.
這使我想起一些歐洲城市的舊城。

A That comparison is pretty close.
這個比較很貼切。

B Can we visit some historical buildings here?
我們在這裡可以參觀一些有歷史的建築物嗎?

A You have quite a lot to choose from.
你有很多選擇。

B What would you suggest first?
你會首先推薦哪一個?

A The 400-year old Longshan Temple.
有四百年歷史的龍山寺。

B Please lead the way.
請帶路吧。

Ⓐ 常說的話

Lugang was founded in the early eighteenth century.
鹿港是十八世紀初所建的。

At that time, Lugang was one of the busiest ports in Taiwan.
在那時候,鹿港是台灣最繁忙的港口之一。

Visitors enjoy taking a walk along the winding alleys in Lugang.
觀光客喜歡在鹿港蜿蜒的巷子內散步。

The Longshan Temple in Lugang is about four hundred years old.
鹿港的龍山寺約有四百年歷史。

The Ding Mansion is a good example of the traditional Chinese architecture.
丁家古厝是傳統中國建築的好例子。

The Folk Arts Museum in Lugang was once the ancestral mansion of the Koo Family.
鹿港民俗文物館曾是辜家祖宅。

You can see the lifestyle of a rich family from late 19th to early 20th century.
你可以看見十九世紀末到二十世紀初富裕人家的生活風格。

A collection of Ming and Ching Dynasty antiques are shown in the museum.
在這文物館內可以見到明朝和清朝的古董收藏。

跟老外介紹台灣這本全包了

track 跨頁共同導讀 055

ⓑ常說的話

What makes Lugang a special historical town?
鹿港為何是個特別的歷史小鎮？

Is the Longshan Temple in Lugang similar to that in Taipei?
鹿港的龍山寺和台北的很相似嗎？

These winding alleys look pretty but are hard to walk.
這些蜿蜒的巷子看來很美，但是很難走。

Can you believe this used to be a family's mansion?
你能相信這曾是某家的豪宅？

Even a place where a family lived could be turned into a museum.
即使是某家族住過的地方也能變為一個文物館。

The Folk Arts Museum in Lugang really opens my eyes.
鹿港民俗文物館真是讓我大開眼界。

To me, Ding Mansion has a unique and outstanding look.
在我看來，丁家古厝有種獨特且超凡的外觀。

I'm very curious about the Glass Museum in Lugang.
我對鹿港玻璃博物館很好奇。

Unit 4
Baguashan Giant Buddha Scenic Area
八卦山大佛風景區

056 track

Baguashan Giant Buddha is the landmark of Changhua.
八卦山大佛風景區是彰化的地標。

情境對話 1

A Now we are standing at an excellent point.
現在我們正站在一個極佳的地點。

B How come this spot is so special?
為何這地點如此特別？

A On this side you can see the giant Buddha.
在這一邊你可以看見大佛。

B And on the other side?
那在另一邊呢？

A Why don't you turn around and take a look?
你怎麼不自己轉個身看看呢？

B Wow! Is this the entire Changhua City?
哇！這是彰化市全景嗎？

跟老外介紹台灣這本全包了

track 跨頁共同導讀 056

●情境對話2

A Can you see the giant black statue of the Buddha over there?
你可以看見在那邊的黑色大佛嗎？

B The statue is so tall that we can see it from far away while driving.
那雕像這麼高，我們老遠就可以在車裡看見了。

A Let's take an uphill walk to the entrance gate of the Giant Buddha Scenic Area.
我們走上坡到八卦山大佛風景區的入口大門。

B This entrance gate is designed very well.
這入口大門的設計很好。

A See these stone Guanyin statues standing around?
你看到了在周圍矗立的觀音石像嗎？

B They all look very kind and respectable.
他們看來都很慈祥、很受人尊敬。

A Now look up and you see the huge Buddha watching over you.
現在你向上看，就會看見大佛觀注著你。

B We're very blessed to have the huge Buddha watching over us.
我們很幸運有大佛觀注著我們。

1
3
8

Ⓐ 常說的話

Once you enter the gate, you are at Baguashan Giant Buddha Scenic Area.
你一進入大門,就進入了八卦山大佛風景區。

The 22-meter black statue of the Buddha is very magnificent.
這座二十二公尺高的黑色佛像非常壯觀。

The gigantic statue of Buddha sits on a huge lotus flower.
這座巨大的佛像坐在一朵大蓮花上。

The giant Buddha watches over Changhua City.
大佛觀注著彰化市。

The story of the Buddha is shown in the eight floors inside the statue.
佛陀的故事展示於佛像內的八層樓中。

Walking up the long uphill path to the big Buddha is symbolic.
走一大段上坡路到大佛,這很有寓意。

The peaceful Buddha stands in contrast to the busy life of Changhua City.
安詳的佛像和彰化市繁忙的生活成了明顯對比。

In the scenic area, various function rooms are open for different groups.
在風景區內有針對不同團體的多功能房間。

跟老外介紹台灣這本全包了

track 跨頁共同導讀 057

B 常說的話

This black giant Buddha seems to be smiling at us.
這座黑色大佛似乎在對我們微笑。

It's nice to have such a huge Buddha watching over the whole city.
有這座大佛觀注整個城市真好。

The giant Buddha can make you feel at ease somehow.
這座大佛似乎能讓你感到自在。

What do these 32 stone Guanyin sculptures mean here?
這三十二座觀音雕像在這裡有什麼意義?

Can you explain the story of the Buddha in English to me?
你能用英語解釋佛陀的故事給我聽嗎?

Many Asian countries I've been to have huge statues of the Buddha.
很多我到過的亞洲城市,都有大佛雕像。

Do most Taiwanese believe in Buddhism?
大多數台灣人信仰佛教嗎?

Do many Taiwanese look for spiritual growth in Buddhism?
很多台灣人轉向佛教尋找精神方面的成長嗎?

Unit 5　Sun Moon Lake
日月潭

Sun Moon Lake offers many beautiful scenes.
日月潭提供許多的美景。

● 情境對話 1 ●

Ⓐ Sun Moon Lake is right in front of us.
日月潭就在我們眼前。

Ⓑ All of a sudden, I feel so calm.
突然之間，我覺得很平靜。

Ⓐ Without the mist, we can see almost all the mountains.
沒有霧的情形下，我們幾乎能看見所有的山群。

Ⓑ And their reflections on the lake.
還有山在湖面上的倒影。

Ⓐ The sun will soon set.
太陽很快就會下山了。

Ⓑ The sunset over the lake is sure to be fantastic.
湖上的夕陽一定很美。

track 跨頁共同導讀 058

●情境對話2●

A This is the largest lake in Taiwan, Sun Moon Lake.
這是日月潭，台灣最大的湖泊。

B Why is the lake called "Sun Moon Lake"?
為什麼這個湖叫作「日月潭」？

A The eastern part of the lake is round like the sun, and the western side is shaped like a crescent moon.
湖的東側像太陽般圓，而湖的西側形狀像新月。

B We should take time to soak in the peace of nature.
我們該慢慢沉浸於大自然的平靜中。

A The scenery of the lake varies according to time and seasons.
這個湖的景色隨著時間和季節而改變。

B The mist also plays an important role, right?
霧也扮演重要的角色，對吧？

A That's why so many people like to stay here for quite a while.
那就是為什麼那麼多人喜歡在這兒待上好一陣子。

B Why don't we stay here for a couple of days, too?
那我們何不也在這兒待個兩三天？

TAIWAN Let's Go!

059 track

ⓐ 常說的話

Sun Moon Lake in Nantou County is the largest lake of Taiwan.
日月潭位於南投,是台灣最大的湖泊。

The Lalu Island is in the middle of the lake.
拉魯島位於湖的中央。

The green reflection of the surrounding mountains is enchanting.
周圍群山的綠色倒影很迷人。

Would you like to ride a bike along the road around the lake?
你想要騎自行車繞湖一週嗎?

Cruising on the lake might be easier for us than rowing a boat.
搭船遊湖對我們而言或許會比划船容易。

It would be great to meditate at the lake side in the morning.
清晨在湖邊冥想會很不錯。

The architecture of the Lalu Hotel is simple yet elegant.
涵碧樓的建築簡單但很優雅。

The Tsou tribe has only over 500 members and is the smallest indigenous group.
鄒族只有五百多人,是人數最少的原住民族。

跟老外介紹台灣這本全包了

track 跨頁共同導讀 059

Ⓑ常說的話●

Sun Moon Lake with morning mist looks very mystical to me.
晨霧中的日月潭對我而言非常神秘。

The beauty of the lake at sunset is beyond words.
筆墨難以形容夕陽中的湖色之美。

Admiring the mountains and lake from a cruising boat is very relaxing.
搭船在湖中欣賞湖光山色,非常令人放鬆。

While you meditate here, I'm going to cycle around Sun Moon Lake.
你在這兒冥想,我要騎自行車繞日月潭一週。

Look at those people doing yoga in the water in front of the Lalu Hotel!
你看那些在涵碧樓前的水裡做瑜珈的人!

Is Sun Moon Lake originally inhabited by the Tsou people?
鄒族人是最先在日月潭居住的人嗎?

Does the name "Lalu" come from the Tsou language?
「拉魯」這名字是出自鄒族語言嗎?

Is it possible to learn about the Tsou culture here?
可以在這兒學習鄒族文化嗎?

144

Unit 6 Xitou 溪頭

060 track

Green shower in Xitou is so refreshing.
在溪頭的森林浴真能提振精神。

情境對話 1

A In a few minutes we'll reach the divine tree.
再過幾分鐘我們就會抵達神木。

B Why is it called a divine tree?
為什麼叫作神木?

A It's an ancient tree that is almost empty inside.
那是棵古老的樹,樹中間幾乎中空。

B How old is it exactly?
確切來說有多老?

A It's about two thousand years old with a huge rock inside.
大約兩千年這麼老,樹中間有塊巨石。

B That sounds like an amazing tree!
聽起來真是棵神奇的樹!

情境對話2

A How I wish I had a back garden like Xitou!
但願溪頭是我家後花園!

B If this were the view from the windows of my room...
要是這是從我房間看出去的景色要多好…

A It's almost impossible to describe to others how beautiful Xitou is.
溪頭之美幾乎難以用筆墨形容。

B They have to actually be here to feel it.
非要身歷其境才能感受。

A The wooden houses here have the natural smell.
這裡的小木屋聞起來很自然。

B I know you love natural things, not man-made.
我知道你喜歡天然的,非人造的東西。

A It's hard to find a house all made of natural wood.
要找間全用天然木頭做的木屋,很不容易。

B Especially these days in a crowded city of tall buildings.
特別是在當今高樓林立的擁擠都市中。

Ⓐ 常說的話

Xitou Nature Education Area is located in central Taiwan's Naitou County.
溪頭自然教育園區位於台灣中部的南投縣。

"Xitou" means the origin of the river (Beishi River).
「溪頭」的意思是溪的源頭（北勢溪）。

The wooden houses in Xitou smell natural and are cozy.
溪頭的木屋聞起來很自然，而且很舒適。

Many couples come to the University Pond for wedding photos.
很多準夫妻來到大學池拍婚紗照。

We can look down from the unique "Corridor in the Air" in the forest.
我們可以從這森林中獨特的「空中步道」向下看。

You'll notice the abundance of the natural life, including birds, insects, and plants.
你會注意到豐富的自然生態，包括鳥、昆蟲和植物。

Can you imagine this divine tree is about two thousand years old?
你能想像這棵神木有約兩千年這麼老嗎？

Xitou is part of the National Taiwan University Experimental Forest.
溪頭是國立台灣大學實驗林的一部分。

跟老外介紹台灣這本全包了

track 跨頁共同導讀 061

Ⓑ常說的話

Xitou is a perfect place to escape the summer heat.
溪頭是避暑的最佳地方。

So far I've learned in Xitou a lot about the nature in central Taiwan.
到現在我在溪頭學到了很多台灣中部的大自然。

In the forest in Xitou, I thoroughly enjoyed a green shower.
在溪頭的森林,我徹底享受了森林浴。

A walk in the woods clears up the thoughts in my mind.
在森林中散步讓我的思緒清晰了許多。

This is my first time to see the "Corridor in the Air".
這是我第一次看到「空中步道」。

Can you take a photo of me in front of the University Pond?
你可以幫我在大學池前拍張照片嗎?

After living in Xitou a couple of days, it is hard to go back to the city life.
在溪頭住了幾天後,很難回到都市生活。

In the States, I've never heard of trees that are as old as the divine tree here.
在美國我從來沒聽過像這裡的神木這麼老的樹木。

Unit 7 Qingjing Farm
清境農場

062 track

Qingjing Farm is a great weekend getaway.
清境農場是週末的最佳去處。

● 情境對話 1

A Do you want to see a sheep-shearing show?
你想看剪羊毛秀嗎?

B Absolutely.
當然。

A A shearer from New Zealand is doing the show here.
一個紐西蘭的剪羊毛人在那兒表演。

B Look at the sheep walking on the stage.
你看那些走上表演台的羊。

A They don't seem to know what's going on.
似乎完全不知道發生了什麼事。

B This sheep shearing show attracts all kids, big and small.
這個剪羊毛秀吸引了大大小小的孩子。

❹ 中部風景區

track 跨頁共同導讀 062

● 情境對話 2

Ⓐ How do you like the mountain air at Qingjing Farm?
你喜歡清境農場的山中空氣嗎？

Ⓑ It is so fresh and cool.
這真清新、真涼爽。

Ⓐ Qingjing Farm is the only farm in Taiwan that is situated in the mountains.
清境農場是台灣唯一位於山中的農場。

Ⓑ What do they grow mostly?
他們大都種些什麼呢？

Ⓐ It differs from one season to another.
隨季節有所不同。

Ⓑ What are some of the typical seasonal produce?
有哪些典型的當季作物？

Ⓐ Flowers in spring, fruits in summer, maple trees in autumn and vegetables in winter.
春天種花，夏天種水果，秋天種楓樹以及冬天種蔬菜。

Ⓑ Of course, we won't forget the sheep and goats.
當然不能忘了綿羊和山羊。

Ⓐ 常說的話

Qingjing Farm is situated in the Ren'ai township of Nantou County.
清境農場位於南投縣仁愛鄉。

Qingjing Farm is the only farm in Taiwan that sits in the high mountains.
清境農場是台灣唯一位於高山的農場。

The mountain air gets fresher and lighter as we hike up.
隨著我們爬得越高，山中空氣就越清新越稀薄。

The sheep-shearing show was run by someone from New Zealand.
剪羊毛秀是由一個紐西蘭人表演的。

The horse-riding show is just as popular as sheep show.
騎馬秀和剪羊毛秀幾乎同樣受歡迎。

Sheep and goats are grazing in the meadow here.
綿羊和山羊在這裡的草地上吃草。

We should try their organic cabbages at Qingjing Farm.
我們該嚐嚐看清境農場的有機高麗菜。

Life at Qingjing Farm is healthier than in a crowded city.
清境農場和擁擠都市的生活比起來，健康太多了。

track 跨頁共同導讀 063

Ⓑ常說的話●

Walking at Qingjing Farm is like walking in the clouds.
在清境農場上散步就像在雲中漫步。

A farm so high in the mountains is rare in the States.
在美國很少有在這樣高山中的農場。

That sheep shearer from New Zealand yelled some words in Chinese.
那個紐西蘭剪羊毛人用中文喊了幾個字。

The audience is concentrating on the sheep-shearing show.
觀眾正專心看剪羊毛秀。

It's interesting to watch flocks of sheep grazing on the grassland.
看一群群的羊在草地上吃草,很有意思。

The organic cabbages taste fresh and slightly sweet.
有機高麗菜吃起來很新鮮,帶點甜味。

Do you think I should buy the mountain tea leaves to take home?
你覺得我該買高山茶葉帶回家嗎?

We should spend more weekends at the farm.
我們該多來這農場渡週末。

Unit 8

Aowanda National Forest Recreation Area
奧萬大國家森林遊樂區

Aowanda is the hometown of maple trees.
奧萬大是楓葉的故鄉。

情境對話 1

A Aren't these red maple leaves pretty?
這些紅楓很美吧。

B We should have someone take a photo of us with the maple trees.
我們該請人幫我們和楓樹照張相。

A From December to next January is the maple season.
從十二月到次年一月是賞楓季節。

B Is it the time for maple leaves to turn red?
那時候楓葉會變紅嗎？

A You are right about it.
你說對了。

B That's when the maple trees are most beautiful.
那時候的楓葉最美不過了。

情境對話 2

A Have you noticed the maple leaves have all turned red?
你注意到所有的楓葉都變紅了嗎？

B There is the breeze that comes through the branches.
樹梢中有微風吹來。

A Just walking through the maple trees makes me feel so good.
光是在楓樹林中散步，就使我感到很舒服。

B I like to enjoy the sunshine and cool air around the maple trees.
我喜歡在這些楓樹周圍享受陽光和涼爽的空氣。

A Some call it Green Shower.
有人稱之為森林浴。

B Does that mean taking a walk in green trees?
那是指在綠樹中散步嗎？

A Most people do some easy exercises and take deep breaths at the same time.
大部分人同時做些簡單的運動，並且深呼吸。

B Green Shower in maple trees suits me perfect now.
在楓樹中做森林浴對我現在再適合不過了。

Ⓐ 常說的話

Aowanda is the best place for watching red maple leaves.
奧萬大是賞紅楓的最佳地點。

Pine trees are as pretty as maple trees here.
這裡的松樹和楓樹一樣美。

Bird watching is popular here from November to next June.
從十一月到次年六月是賞鳥的好季節。

Many people come here to watch fireflies as well.
很多人來這兒也看螢火蟲。

Ⓑ 常說的話

I didn't know there were maple trees in Taiwan until now.
現在我才知道台灣有楓樹。

Maple trees here are a lot more beautiful than I thought.
這裡的楓樹比我所想的還要美很多。

Red maple season here only lasts about two months.
這裡的賞楓季只持續約兩個月。

I like to walk on yellow maple leaves on the ground.
我喜歡在枯黃的楓葉道路上走路。

Chapter 5

Southern Scenic Spots
南部風景區

Unit 1 Alishan
阿里山

066 track

The sunrise at Alishan is splendid.
阿里山的日出很輝煌。

●情境對話1●

A What time did the hotel tell us the sun is to rise?
旅館告訴我們日出是什麼時候？

B I think it is 5:05 a.m.
我想是清晨五點五分。

A Get up now! We've got to rush there.
現在快起來！我們得趕到那裡。

B What a fuss about a sunrise!
看日出值得這麼麻煩嗎？

A The sunrise is a must-see in Alishan.
阿里山的日出是必看美景。

B We'll make it just in time.
我們會及時趕到的。

track 跨頁共同導讀 066

●情境對話2●

A After the half-hour train ride, we finally got here in time.
搭了半小時火車,我們總算及時趕到這裡了。

B When is the sun going to rise? I'm starving.
太陽什麼時候會出來?我快餓死了。

A Be patient! So many other visitors are waiting, too.
有點耐心好嗎?這麼多其他遊客也在等。

B Look! The sun is peeking out over there.
看!太陽在那邊露出臉來了。

A Can you imagine how fast the sun is rising?
你能想像日出有這麼快嗎?

B Right now the glorious sun has totally appeared.
現在燦爛的太陽已經完全出現了。

A Look at the sea of clouds.
你看雲海。

B If only I knew how to take a good photo of scenery.
要是我知道如何拍風景照就好了。

Ⓐ 常說的話

Alishan was originally inhabited by the indigenous Tsou people.
阿里山最先是原住民鄒族的居住地。

In the late 18th century, the ethnic Chinese settlers moved into the mountains.
在十八世紀末漢族開墾至山裡。

The Japanese found cypresses in Alishan and started the logging industry there.
日本人在阿里山發現了檜樹，便在那兒開始伐木業。

The Alishan Forest Railway was built to transport lumber.
阿里山森林火車是建來運輸木材的。

In 2001 the area became a national scenic area because of the increasing number of tourists.
因應日漸增多的遊客，2001年建立了國家森林區。

In Alishan, tea and wasabi plantations are very important.
在阿里山，茶葉和山葵是非常重要的農作物。

The sunrise over Yushan can be seen on the eastern peak of Alishan.
在阿里山東邊山頂可以遙望玉山上的日出。

Some giant cypresses in Alishan have been growing for a very long time.
有些阿里山巨大的檜樹樹齡已經很高了。

跟老外介紹台灣這本全包了

track 跨頁共同導讀 067

B 常說的話

I can't wait to see the famous sunrise in Alishan.
我等不及去看阿里山上的日出。

The beautiful sunrise is worth getting up for so early.
這樣美麗的日出值得這麼早起。

The tea grown in Alishan must be quality mountain tea.
阿里山上種的茶一定是優質的高山茶。

Have you tasted wasabi grown in Alishan?
你嚐過阿里山上種的山葵嗎？

We should have worn better sneakers for the wet trails.
我們應該穿好點的球鞋才對，這步道真濕。

They even built the Tree Spirit Pagoda for the old cypresses in Alishan.
他們還建了樹靈塔來保護阿里山的古檜樹。

These two hiking trails here can lead you to the cypresses.
這兩條步道可帶你到檜樹。

Let's check out the Two Sisters Pond in the forest.
我們到姊妹潭去看看。

Unit 2 Anping District, Tainan City
臺南安平

Anping District is a town full of cultural heritage.
臺南安平是個充滿文化古蹟的小鎮。

● 情境對話 1 ●

A This is the famous Anping Fort.
這就是有名的安平古堡。

B Who built it?
誰建的呢？

A This is the first fort the Dutch built in Taiwan.
這是荷蘭人在台灣建立的第一座城堡。

B That must have been a long time ago.
那距今一定很久了。

A Originally it was called "Fort Zeelandia".
原先稱為「熱蘭遮城」。

B Let's check out the stories of the historical fort.
我們來看看這古堡的故事。

track 跨頁共同導讀 068

●情境對話2●

A Eternal Golden Castle is a bit far away from the city.
億載金城離市區有點遠。

B We can't miss this First Grade Historic Site.
我們不能錯過國家一級古蹟。

A Look at the red arched castle gate not far away.
你看不遠處的紅色圓拱城門。

B There is even a river around the fortress.
在堡壘周圍還有一條河。

A This is not something you can find somewhere else in Taiwan.
這在台灣別處是找不到的。

B Was Eternal Golden Castle built by foreigners, too?
億載金城也是外國人所建的嗎？

A It was designed by a French engineer but built by the Chinese.
這是由法國工程師設計，中國人所建的。

B The fortress seems to be telling many stories.
這堡壘似乎在對我們訴說著很多故事。

❹常說的話●

In 1624, the Dutch built the first fort in Anping, called "Fort Zeelandia".
荷蘭人於1624年在安平建立第一座城堡，稱為「熱蘭遮城」。

Fort Zeelandia was once the center of politics and trade in Taiwan.
熱蘭遮城曾是台灣政治和貿易中心。

Anping Fort is now a First Grade Historic Site in Taiwan.
安平古堡現在是國家一級古蹟。

Eternal Golden Castle is a breakthrough in Taiwanese military defense.
億載金城是台灣軍事防禦上的重大突破。

After the restoration, much of the original fortress can be seen now.
重建後的堡壘，原來樣貌現在大致都可以看到。

Through the arched castle gate, you can see a green grass carpet.
從圓拱城門看出去，你可以看到綠色草坪。

The grass carpet at the fortress used to be the exercising field.
堡壘的綠色草坪從前是用來當作運動場地的。

Ⓑ常說的話

How long were the Dutch in this part of Taiwan for?
荷蘭人在台灣這一地區有多久？

What is the meaning of "Zeelandia"?
「熱蘭遮」是什麼意思？

Look at the beautiful sunset at Anping Fort with its red bricks.
你看在美麗夕陽下用紅磚砌成的安平古堡。

The afternoon firing ceremony at Eternal Golden Castle is interesting.
億載金城下午的發砲典禮很有意思。

Who is the person of the brass statue of at the fortress?
堡壘的銅像是誰？

A visit to Eternal Golden Castle is worth the trip.
億載金城值得一遊。

You'll like posing in front of the old cannons for a photo.
你會喜歡在古砲前拍張相片。

Tainan is a historical city of Taiwan.
台南是個充滿台灣歷史的城市。

Unit 3　Tainan Confucius Temple
臺南孔廟

070 track

You'll enjoy a visit to Tainan Confucius Temple.
你會喜歡參觀臺南孔廟。

● 情境對話 1

A Let me show you Tainan Confucius Temple.
讓我帶你參觀臺南孔廟。

B To be honest, I'm not a fan of heritage.
老實說，我不是非常喜歡古蹟。

A You don't have to be.
你不必非常喜歡古蹟。

B You mean everyone can enjoy a visit to this temple?
你是說每個人都會喜歡參觀這間廟？

A Certainly, including you.
當然，包括你在內。

B You know I'm very open-minded.
你知道我是個心胸開放的人。

情境對話 2

A You can't come to Tainan without visiting the Confucius Temple.
來到台南而不參觀孔廟是不行的。

B What is so special about this Tainan Confucius Temple?
臺南孔廟為何那麼特別？

A It is the first Confucius temple built in Taiwan.
那是台灣最早建立的孔廟。

B It must have gone through reconstruction many times.
那一定經歷了很多次的改建。

A Each renovation was carefully recorded in the temple.
每次裝修都仔細紀錄在廟內。

B This shows great efforts have been put into the preservation.
這表示維修工程不遺餘力。

A We can see the traditional Confucius ceremony performed here.
在這裡我們可以看到傳統的祭孔典禮。

B Can we be the audience of the ceremony today?
我們今天能觀禮嗎？

Ⓐ常說的話

Tainan Confucius Temple was built in 1666.
臺南孔廟建於 1666 年。

That was the first Confucius Temple and the "Highest Institute" in Taiwan.
那是台灣最早的孔廟和「最高學府」。

The style of Tainan Confucius Temple is simple and elegant.
臺南孔廟的風格簡單但優雅。

The Confucius Temple has been renovated more than thirty times.
孔廟改建了三十多次。

The divine tablets of Confucius are housed in the temple.
孔廟匾額收藏於廟內。

Tainan Confucius Temple is, of course, a First Grade Historic Site.
臺南孔廟當然是國家一級古蹟。

The government has worked hard to preserve the artifacts of the temple.
政府致力於廟內文物的保存。

The National Museum of Taiwan Literature is very close to the Confucius Temple.
國立台灣文學館離孔廟很近。

B 常說的話

Is Confucianism still deeply rooted in education here?
儒家思想仍然深植於這裡的教育嗎?

Are the Confucius ceremonies conducted every day in the temple?
每天都有祭孔典禮在廟內舉行嗎?

Look at the bright ritual costumes in the Confucius ceremony.
你看祭孔典禮上的鮮豔禮服。

The musical instruments in the ceremony must have a long history.
典禮上所用的樂器想必歷史悠久。

They say the Confucius ceremonies are exactly the same as in the past.
聽說祭孔典禮和從前完全一樣。

As you said, the Confucius Temple itself is a site of traditional culture.
如同你所說的,孔廟本身就是傳統文化所在地。

In the States, it would be really difficult to find a place like this.
在美國要想找到像這樣的地方很難。

I've heard a lot about the National Museum of Taiwan Literature.
我聽說了很多關於國立台灣文學館的事。

Unit 4 The Love River
愛河

072 track

The Love River is significant to Kaohsiung.
愛河對高雄很重要。

● 情境對話 1 ●

A Want to take a boat trip down the Love River?
你想要搭船遊愛河嗎？

B What can I see along the boat trip?
在船上可以看見什麼呢？

A The Love River that runs through Kaohsiung.
流經高雄的愛河。

B Can we see the whole of Kaohsiung from the river?
遊河過程可以看見整個高雄嗎？

A Pretty much so.
差不多可以。

B That's what I call a boat trip.
搭船旅遊就該如此。

❺ 南部風景區

情境對話2

A Taking an evening walk along the Love River is wonderful.
傍晚在愛河旁散步真好。

B I can feel the cool breeze in the evening.
我可以感受到涼爽的晚風。

A During the daytime, it was a little too warm.
白天有點太熱。

B Look over there! A live band is performing in the park.
你看那兒!公園內有個樂團在現場表演。

A In the parks near the Love River, there are always some events.
在愛河旁的公園總有些活動在進行。

B Let's go there and listen to their rock music.
我們去那兒聽搖滾樂吧。

A There is also a night market with many food stands.
那兒還有個攤販聚集的夜市。

B Nothing compares to eating while standing in a rock concert.
一邊吃一邊站著聽搖滾音樂會,沒有什麼比這樣更好了。

Ⓐ常說的話

The Love River is a 12-kilometer long river in southern Taiwan.
愛河是條位於南台灣,有 12 公里長的河。

The Love River runs through Kaohsiung City to Kaohsiung Harbor.
愛河流經高雄市,於高雄港入海。

Lovers enjoy walking along the river, and that's why it's called the Love River.
情侶喜歡在河邊散步,因此這條河被稱為愛河。

The Love River is culturally and economically significant to Kaohsiung.
愛河對高雄在文化和經濟上很重要。

There are several riverside parks along the Love River.
愛河旁有好幾個河濱的公園。

Live concerts and night markets are often held in the riverside parks.
河濱的公園內常有現場演奏和夜市。

Wouldn't you like to take the boat to go down the river?
你一定很想搭船遊河吧?

Recently the city government cleaned up the Love River.
最近市政府將愛河整治乾淨。

Ⓑ常說的話

The Love River is the spine of Kaohsiung.
愛河可說是高雄的脊椎。

The boat trip on the Love River was very impressive to me.
搭船遊愛河令我印象深刻。

Some events are going on in the riverside parks.
河濱的公園內有些活動在進行。

The night scenery of the Love River is fascinating.
愛河晚間的景色真是迷人。

Look at the bright lighting reflected on the Love River.
看看愛河上反射出的鮮豔光芒。

The atmosphere along the river is really suitable for lovers.
河邊的氣氛真的很適合情侶。

People of all ages like the Love River and the riverside parks.
所有年紀的人都喜歡愛河和河濱的公園。

The Love River must be full of old stories of Kaohsiung.
愛河想必充滿高雄的古老故事。

Unit 5 Qijin
旗津

Qijin is a narrow island near Kaohsiung.
旗津是靠近高雄的狹長島嶼。

情境對話 1

A Do you still remember Mazu?
你還記得媽祖嗎?

B Isn't that the goddess of the sea you told me?
那不就是你告訴過我的海神嗎?

A Yes, the Tianhou Temple at Qijin worships Mazu.
是的,旗津的天后宮供奉媽祖。

B I can imagine most people at Qijin live on the sea.
我可以想像大部分的旗津人靠海為生。

A The Tianhou Temple is a historic site.
天后宮是個歷史古蹟。

B Our next stop will be the Mazu Temple at Qijin.
我們下一站就去旗津的媽祖宮。

情境對話 2

track 跨頁共同導讀 074

A You're going to love Qijin because you are a fan of seafood.
你會很喜歡旗津的,因為你是海鮮饕客。

B How long will this boat trip to Qijin take?
船開到旗津需要多久時間?

A It'll take only 30 minutes.
只要三十分鐘。

B For fantastic seafood, I'm willing to go anywhere anyhow.
為了美味海鮮,我不計代價。

A We'll go to Old Street as soon as we reach Qijin.
我們一到旗津,就會去老街。

B Can we find many good seafood restaurants on the street?
在那條街上可以找到很多很好的海鮮餐廳嗎?

A The whole street is full of seafood eateries and stands.
整條街都是海鮮店和攤販。

B Right now I have this picture of grilled scallop in my head.
現在我的腦海中浮現出烤干貝。

A 常說的話

Qijin is a narrow island southwest of Kaohsiung.
旗津是高雄西南的狹長島嶼。

Qijin Island was once connected to Taiwan Island but not anymore.
旗津島曾經與台灣相連,但是現在沒有了。

The Cross Harbor Tunnel connects Qijin Island to Kaohsiung.
跨海隧道連接旗津島與高雄。

Two ferries take you to Qijin at the northern top and the middle of the island.
兩個渡輪能分別帶你到旗津島的北部和中部。

On Qijin Old Street, many restaurants sell fresh seafood outdoors.
在旗津老街有很多餐廳在戶外賣新鮮的海鮮。

The Tianhou Temple worships Mazu and is also called the Mazu Temple.
天后宮拜媽祖,又稱媽祖宮。

You can get a bird's-eye view of Kaohsiung Harbor from the lighthouse.
從這燈塔你可以鳥瞰高雄港。

We should go to the Qijin Seashore Park to see their seashells.
我們該到旗津海岸公園看他們收藏的貝殼。

跟老外介紹台灣這本全包了

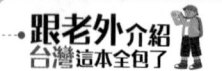

track 跨頁共同導讀 075

Ⓑ 常說的話

I prefer to take the ferries from Kaohsiung to Qijin Island.
我比較喜歡從高雄搭渡輪到旗津島。

You can see the whole Kaohsiung Harbor from the lighthouse.
從這燈塔可以看見整個高雄港。

From this lighthouse, you get to see what you usually don't see.
從這燈塔你可以看見一般看不到的景色。

It's not hard to understand why people at Qijin worship Mazu.
不難理解為何旗津人祭拜媽祖。

The whole Old Street is lined with seafood restaurants.
整條老街都是海鮮餐廳。

The scenery on Qijin Island has the flavor of southern Taiwan.
旗津島的風景有南台灣風情。

Why don't we spend some time at the Qijin Seashore Park?
我們何不去旗津海岸公園逛逛呢？

The seashells collected here reflect the rich creatures in the sea.
這兒收藏的貝殼反應出豐富的海洋生態。

176

Unit 6 Xizi Bay
西子灣

076 track

The sunset in Xizi Bay is spectacular.
西子灣的夕陽很美。

● 情境對話 1

A The sun is about to go down.
太陽快西下了。

B All these people here are watching it.
這兒所有的人都在看。

A In Xizi Bay, the sunset is said to be especially beautiful.
聽說西子灣的夕陽特別美。

B Look! Little by little the sun is disappearing.
看！太陽一點一點消失中。

A The red sea of clouds is also glorious.
火紅的雲海也很燦爛。

B The sun will soon set.
太陽就快西下了。

❺ 南部風景區

情境對話 2

A This time we have a white sand beach in Xizi Bay.
這次我們在西子灣會有白沙灘。

B That's what I've dreamed of for a long while.
那就是我一直渴望的。

A This beach with coconut palms is well-maintained.
這個種滿椰子樹的海灘維護得很好。

B Just take a look at the scenery and clear blue water.
看看這風景和清澈蔚藍的海水。

A The beach also features colorful coral reefs.
同時也有多彩多姿的珊瑚礁。

B It's so close to the crowded center of Kaohsiung City.
離擁擠的高雄市中心這麼近。

A Over here we can do all sorts of beach activities.
在這兒我們可以從事各式各樣的海灘活動。

B First of all, let's beat these guys playing volleyball.
首先,讓我們先來打敗這些玩排球的傢伙吧。

Ⓐ 常說的話

Xizi Bay is located at the western edge of Kaohsiung City.
西子灣位於高雄市的西岸。

Xizi Bay is well-known for its blue water and sand beaches.
西子灣以蔚藍海水和沙灘聞名。

Many people enjoy playing volleyball and swimming here.
很多人喜歡在這兒玩排球和游泳。

Isn't it great to just bathe under the sun in Xizi Bay?
在西子灣作日光浴很舒服吧?

Some come to Xizi Bay just to hang out at the beach.
有些人來西子灣只是為了要在海灘上逛逛。

Watching sunset in Xizi Bay is a favorite activity for many people.
在西子灣看夕陽是很多人喜歡的活動。

These coconut palms give people the atmosphere of a vacation.
這些椰子樹給人渡假的氣氛。

People come to Xizi Bay mainly to spend leisure time.
來西子灣的人主要為了休閒。

B 常說的話

People in Kaohsiung are lucky to have Xizi Bay.
住在高雄的人有西子灣真幸運。

Xizi Bay is the kind of beach we all want close to where we live.
大家都會希望,在自家附近就有個像西子灣一樣的海灘。

I feel like we are on vacation with the coconut palms on the sand beach.
我感到我們像在椰子樹下的沙灘上渡假。

Let's join these girls to play volleyball with them!
讓我們加入這些女孩,和他們玩排球吧!

The sunset in Xizi Bay is truly special and spectacular.
西子灣的夕陽真的很特別很美。

They are all waiting to watch the sun going down.
他們都在等著看夕陽西下。

What more can you ask for?
真是再好不過了。

It's good to feel the soft cool breeze in the air.
溫柔涼爽的晚風吹來,感覺真好。

Unit 7 Kenting
墾丁

Kenting has tropical climate and great scenery.
墾丁有熱帶氣候和美好風景。

● 情境對話 1 ●

A Now we are in the Kenting National Park.
現在我們位於墾丁國家公園。

B Are we now in the tropical area?
現在我們在熱帶地區嗎?

A Yes, you can tell it from the plants around you.
是的,你可以從周圍的植物看出來。

B Is there a white sand beach in the national park?
在國家公園內有白色的沙灘嗎?

A Sure. There is this "Baishawan" for all water sports.
當然。有一個可做各種水上運動的「白沙灣」。

B What are we waiting for? Let's go!
那我們還在等什麼?走吧!

跟老外介紹台灣這本全包了

track 跨頁共同導讀 078

情境對話 1

A Do you know "Spring Scream" is held every year here?
你知道「春天吶喊」每年都在這裡舉行嗎?

B What is "Spring Scream" after all?
到底什麼是「春天吶喊」?

A It is an outdoor rock-band festival held in April each year.
那是個每年四月舉行的戶外搖滾音樂季。

B It sounds like an event for young people, like us.
聽起來像是給像我們這樣年輕人的活動。

A The event can last as long as 11 days.
這個活動可以持續十一天。

B What else do they do in "Spring Scream"?
「春天吶喊」還有什麼活動?

A There are films, art exhibitions, DJs, camping and so on.
還有電影、藝術展覽、DJ、露營等等。

B Make sure we register in advance for the next one.
下一次我們一定要提早報名。

Ⓐ 常說的話

Kenting National Park was the first national park of Taiwan.
墾丁國家公園是台灣的第一個國家公園。

Kenting National Park covers the southernmost area of Taiwan.
墾丁國家公園涵蓋台灣最南部的地區。

With sunshine and tropical climate, Kenting attracts lots of tourists.
墾丁有陽光和熱帶氣候，吸引了無數觀光客。

You can see many mountains and coral reefs along the coasts.
你可以看見很多山和岸邊的珊瑚礁。

Ⓑ 常說的話

This is my first time to visit a national park with a tropical climate.
這是我第一次到熱帶的國家公園玩。

Can we take part in the next "Spring Scream"?
我們可以參加下次的「春天吶喊」嗎？

Is it possible to dive near the coral coasts in Kenting?
能在墾丁的珊瑚岸邊潛水嗎？

Chapter 6

Eastern Scenic Spots
東部風景區

Unit 1

Taroko Gorge
太魯閣峽谷

Taroko Gorge is magnificent and splendid.
太魯閣峽谷真是雄偉壯麗。

● 情境對話 1 ●

A Now you know we've arrived at Taroko Gorge.
現在你知道我們到了太魯閣峽谷。

B It is such an impressive canyon.
真是令人印象深刻的峽谷。

A Look at the steep cliffs all over there.
你看那邊那些陡峭的懸崖。

B It must have taken ages for the cliffs to become that way.
那些峭壁一定是經過很久時間才變成那樣。

A The best way for us to enjoy the views is hiking.
我們最好的賞景方式是健行。

B I totally agree with you on that.
這點我完全同意。

情境對話 2

A Every time I am at Taroko Gorge, I appreciate it even more than before.
每次來到太魯閣峽谷,都令我更加讚嘆不已。

B I don't have the right words to describe its beauty.
我沒有辦法用筆墨來形容這美景。

A It is the sheer work of Nature.
這純粹是大自然的傑作。

B Who wouldn't want to hike all the trails to admire the gorge?
誰不會想要走遍所有登山步道,來觀賞峽谷?

A Thanks to the Central Cross-Island Highway, we are able to get here.
由於中部橫貫公路的開通,我們才得以來到這裡。

B Let's visit the Eternal Spring Shrine, which you mentioned before.
我們去參觀你提過的長春祠吧。

A You are absolutely right about this.
你說的真有理。

B We should thank those indigenous people who were here before us, too.
我們也應該感謝那些比我們先到這裡的原住民。

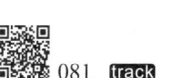

Ⓐ 常說的話

In the language of the Truku people, "Taroko" means magnificent.
在太魯閣族語,「太魯閣」是雄偉壯麗的意思。

The 19-km-long gorge with steep cliffs is right near Taiwan's east coast.
這個十九公尺長的峽谷,有著懸崖峭壁,緊鄰台灣的東岸。

As you can see, the geological wonders of Taroko Gorge are astonishing.
如你所能見到的,太魯閣峽谷的地理奇景非常驚人。

From this point, you have the best view of the gorge.
從這裡你能看見峽谷最佳景觀。

I hope we'll see rare animals and plants indigenous to Taiwan.
希望我們會看見台灣稀有的原生動植物。

Taroko Gorge is mostly inhabited by indigenous people.
太魯閣峽谷地區大多是原住民所居住的。

There are many hiking trails here for you to choose from.
這裡有很多健行步道讓你挑選。

Hiking is the ideal way to see all of Taroko Gorge.
想看遍太魯閣峽谷,健行是個理想方式。

跟老外介紹台灣這本全包了

track 跨頁共同導讀 081

Ⓑ常說的話

I've never seen steep cliffs and natural huge rocks like these.
我從來沒看過像這樣的峭壁和天然巨石。

Words fail to describe the beauty of Taroko Gorge.
無法用筆墨來形容太魯閣峽谷之美。

The natural beauty left me speechless and in awe.
這自然美景令我啞口無言、心生敬畏。

My skills of photography can't capture the beauty of Taroko Gorge.
我的攝影技術無法捕捉太魯閣峽谷之美。

I suppose the best way to enjoy sightseeing here is by foot.
我猜在這裡最佳的賞景方式是步行的方式。

What is Eternal Spring Shrine built for?
長春祠是為何而建的?

Where can we learn about the indigenous culture here?
我們在哪裡可以瞭解到這裡的原住民文化?

Let's see if we can spot the rare animals here.
看我們是否能看到這裡的稀有動物。

Unit 2 Carp Lake 鯉魚潭

Pedaling on Carp Lake is easy and fun.
在鯉魚潭踩腳踏船簡單又好玩。

情境對話 1

A How do you feel pedaling on Carp Lake now?
現在你覺得在鯉魚潭踩腳踏船如何？

B I would appreciate it if you would pedal a bit harder.
要是你能踩得更用力一點，我會感激不盡。

A I think I am doing my share of work very well.
我認為我這部分的工作做得很好。

B How can you be so sure?
你怎麼能如此確定？

A I have come to Carp Lake to pedal since I was small.
我很小的時候就來過鯉魚潭踩腳踏船。

B If so, I should work harder on this.
要是這樣的話，我該要更努力些。

track 跨頁共同導讀 082

情境對話 2

A My parents used to let us pedal on Carp Lake.
我父母曾經讓我們來鯉魚潭踩腳踏船過。

B Did they tell you where the name "Carp Lake" comes from?
他們告訴過你「鯉魚潭」這名字的由來嗎?

A No, they didn't, and I guess they didn't know then.
沒有,我猜他們那時不知道。

B Do you think it is because there are lots of carps in the lake?
你覺得會不會是因為湖內有很多鯉魚?

A That's the first reason; the second reason is that the mountain nearby is carp-shaped.
那是第一個原因;第二個原因是附近的山形狀像鯉魚。

B Of course, for these two reasons, the lake is called "Carp Lake".
當然,因為這兩個理由,這個湖叫作「鯉魚潭」。

A Lots of people are having fun pedaling on the lake.
好多人在鯉魚潭享受踩腳踏船。

B Let's join them right away.
我們馬上加入他們吧。

ⒶⒶ常說的話

Carp Lake is situated in the south of Hualien County.
鯉魚潭位於花蓮縣的南部。

The size of the lake varies with the amount of rainfall.
潭水的大小隨著降雨量有所不同。

You can walk or cycle along the 4-kilometer track around the lake.
你可以沿著環湖的四公里車道騎自行車。

It takes about one hour to walk all the way around Carp Lake.
繞鯉魚潭走一圈要約一小時。

Pedal boats can be seen everywhere on the lake on sunny days.
鯉魚潭在晴天時可以到處看見腳踏船。

The lake reflects the surrounding mountains.
潭水映照出周圍山色。

Many people like to picnic and camp near Carp Lake.
很多人喜歡在鯉魚潭附近野餐和露營。

Paragliding has become popular recently in this area.
最近在這地區飛行傘變得很流行。

Ⓑ 常說的話

Let's pedal on the lake while the weather is so good.
趁現在天氣好,我們去踩腳踏船吧。

If it takes only about one hour, we should walk around Carp Lake.
如果只需要一小時,那我們應該繞鯉魚潭走一圈。

Can carp still be found in Carp Lake now?
現在鯉魚潭裡還有鯉魚嗎?

Maybe we can try camping here since it's a sunny day.
既然天氣這麼好,或許我們可以試著在這裡露營。

Over there, I saw people tasting the fresh shrimp from Carp Lake.
我看到那邊有人在品嚐鯉魚潭的新鮮蝦子。

Some say many fireflies are here at night time.
有人說這裡晚上有很多螢火蟲。

Would you like to come to Carp Lake again at night?
你晚上想要再來鯉魚潭一趟嗎?

Would you like to try paragliding near Carp Lake?
你想試試在鯉魚潭附近玩飛行傘嗎?

Unit 3 Hualien City
花蓮市

Hualien is the City of Marble.
花蓮是大理石之都。

情境對話 1

A Marble shops can be found everywhere in Hualien.
大理石商店在花蓮到處可見。

B They are in all shapes and colors.
有各種形狀和顏色。

A Why not pick some marbles to take home?
為何不挑些大理石帶回家?

B This pink marble is polished very fine.
這塊粉紅色的大理石磨得很光滑。

A You can use it as a paperweight.
你可以用這個來當紙鎮。

B That's a good way of using it.
真是好用法。

跟老外介紹台灣這本全包了

track 跨頁共同導讀 084

●情境對話2

A Hualien is home to the Ami and Atayal peoples.
花蓮是阿美族和泰雅族的故鄉。

B Where do these indigenous peoples live nowadays?
這些原住民現今居住於哪裡?

A The Atayal people live in low mountains, and most Ami live near the coast.
泰雅族住在山腳下,大多的阿美族住在海岸邊。

B Do they still live in their traditional ways?
他們仍然保持傳統生活方式嗎?

A Some work in local cement industry, and most of them still work in the countryside.
有些在當地的水泥業工作,大部分人仍然靠農耕維生。

B Where can I see the traditions of these indigenous peoples?
我在哪裡能夠看見這些原住民的傳統呢?

A The Ami Cultural Village is famous for Ami song and dance performances.
阿美文化村以阿美歌舞表演而聞名。

B Please make sure we don't miss it.
我們可別錯過這個。

194

A 常說的話

Hualien is a charming city, with the culture of the indigenous people.
花蓮是個迷人的都市,富有原住民文化。

Hualien is one of the biggest producers of marble in the world.
花蓮是世界最大的大理石生產地之一。

One specialty of Hualien is Mochi, sticky rice cake.
花蓮的一項特產是麻糬,也就是糯米糰。

The prices of the high quality marble are reasonable in Hualien.
花蓮的優質大理石價格很合理。

Many buildings in Hualien are decorated with marble.
很多花蓮的建築物是用大理石作裝飾。

The Harvest Festival is very important to the Ami people.
豐年祭對阿美族非常重要。

Most of the Ami people rely on agriculture to make a living.
大部分阿美族靠農耕維生。

They have a slow and relaxed pace of life in Hualien.
他們在花蓮的生活步調很慢、很悠閒。

track 跨頁共同導讀 085

Ⓑ常說的話

These polished marble eggs are ideal souvenirs from Hualien.
這些磨得光滑的大理石蛋,是花蓮最佳紀念品。

I've never seen sidewalks paved with marble until now.
我還是第一次看到人行道是用大理石鋪的。

High quality marble is very rare where I come from.
優質大理石在我的家鄉很少見。

These Ami song and dance performers are excellent.
這些阿美族歌舞表演非常優秀。

Can I join the Ami Harvest Festival and dance with them?
我可以加入阿美族豐年祭,和他們一起跳舞嗎?

Do you want to try the seafood near the seaport?
你想嚐嚐看海港旁的海鮮嗎?

The Mochi of Hualien is now one of my favorite Taiwanese specialties.
花蓮的麻糬現在是我最喜歡的台灣特產之一。

There are so many things worth seeing and doing in Hualien.
在花蓮有這麼多值得看和值得做的事物。

Unit 4　Xiuguluan River
秀姑巒溪

086 track

You must try rafting on Xiuguluan River.
你應該試試秀姑巒溪泛舟。

●情境對話 1

A Do you want to try something really exciting?
你想要試試看真正刺激的事嗎?

B Like what?
像什麼?

A Have you heard of rafting on Xiuguluan River?
你聽過秀姑巒溪泛舟嗎?

B No, but it sounds like fun, and I am a good swimmer.
沒有,不過聽起來很好玩,而且我泳技很好。

A This time you have to prove yourself excellent in rafting.
這次你得要證明你自己很會泛舟。

B Sign me up!
幫我報名!

情境對話 2

A Watch out for the other rafters splashing at us!
小心那些人正在對我們潑水!

B Don't they have better things to do on the raft?
他們在船上難道沒有別的事好做嗎?

A Splashing is part of the traditions of rafting on Xiuguluan River.
潑水是秀姑巒溪泛舟的傳統之一。

B If that's the case, I am going to splash back at them, too.
要是那樣的話,我也要對他們潑水。

A You'd better do so if you're going to be a good sport.
那樣做最好,如果你要表現得很上道的話。

B I've got to work on my skills of rafting on the rapid currents.
我得要加緊訓練在急流泛舟的技術。

A Very soon you can take part in our biggest rafting competition here.
很快你就可以參加這裡最大型的泛舟比賽了。

B Thank you very much for your encouragement.
多謝你的鼓勵。

Ⓐ 常說的話

Xiuguluan River is the longest river in eastern Taiwan.
秀姑巒溪是東台灣最長的河流。

Rafting on Xiuguluan River is something you don't want to miss.
你不會想要錯過秀姑巒溪泛舟。

We will get grouped with others to make up 7 or 8 people per raft.
我們會和別人被分到七或八人一組的船。

Make sure you get your life jacket strapped on before the raft trip.
開始泛舟前要確定你的救生衣穿好了。

The raft trip lasts from about 10 am to 2 pm, with a lunch break.
泛舟開始於上午約十點，結束於下午兩點，午餐時間有休息。

The raft trip is about 22 km long, and it descends 65 meters.
泛舟行程約二十二公里，高度下降六十五公里。

The first section is easy, and rafters can work on their skills.
第一階段很容易，泛舟者可以練習技巧。

The second section is much harder than the first one and requires more skills.
第二階段比第一階段難很多，需要更多技巧。

track 跨頁共同導讀 087

B 常說的話

How much time will the raft trip take?
泛舟全程要多久?

How long are we going to raft on Xiuguluan river?
我們在秀姑巒溪還要泛舟多久?

I don't understand the safety instructions because there's no English version.
我聽不懂安全指南,因為沒有英文版。

I hope we can get to Qimei soon, so we can have lunch.
我希望我們能快一點到奇美,這樣才能吃午餐。

The post-Qimei part of the river is said to be very challenging.
奇美後的溪流聽說非常有挑戰性。

Why do the other rafters keep splashing at us?
為什麼其他那些泛舟的人一直對我們潑水呢?

That guy is using a bucket to splash at me.
那傢伙一直用水桶對我潑水。

We are lucky to have warm water in the river around this time.
我們真幸運,現在溪流水溫很溫暖。

Unit 5 Ruisui 瑞穗

Ruisui Ranch is a dairy farm worth visiting.
瑞穗牧場是個值得參觀的酪農場。

情境對話 1

A Would you like to feed cows?
你想要餵牛嗎？

B Can I do that in eastern Taiwan?
在東台灣我可以餵牛嗎？

A You can be among cows on Ruisui Ranch.
在瑞穗牧場你可以和牛群在一起。

B Can I see other animals on the ranch?
能見到牧場上的其它動物嗎？

A You will spot a few ostriches there.
你會看到那裡的一些鴕鳥。

B I'd like to experience life on a ranch right now.
我現在很想要體驗牧場生活。

情境對話 2

A How about hiking with me in the Fuyuan National Forest Recreation Area?
你想要跟我去富源國家森林遊樂區健行嗎?

B Is the scenery nearby good enough?
附近的風景夠好嗎?

A We'll be surrounded by birds and butterflies along the hikes.
一路健行下來我們會被鳥和蝴蝶所圍繞。

B Can we actually spot various pretty birds and butterflies?
我們真的能看見不同種類美麗的鳥和蝴蝶嗎?

A Almost all past travelers were lucky enough to see them.
幾乎所有去過的遊客都有幸看到。

B Is there any hot scenic spot in the forest area?
在森林區有什麼熱門景點?

A There is one suspension bridge that the locals often go to.
有個當地人常去的吊橋。

B So much about talking. We should hit the road now.
光說沒用。現在我們該上路了。

089 track

Ⓐ常說的話●

Cows are grazing on the grassland on Ruisui Ranch.
牛在瑞穗牧場的草地上吃草。

On the ranch, you can feed cows as much as you want to.
在牧場上,你可以盡情餵牛。

Many dairy products from Ruisui Ranch are available to visitors.
遊客可以買到很多種瑞穗牧場乳製品。

Cheesecake, milk pudding and milk nougat are the specialties here.
起士蛋糕、牛奶布丁和牛軋糖是這裡的特產。

Some ostriches come to people very closely.
有些鴕鳥會很靠近人。

Fuyuan National Forest Recreation Area is also known as Butterfly Valley.
富源國家森林遊樂區也被稱為蝴蝶谷。

Many birds and butterflies can be seen in Butterfly Valley.
蝴蝶谷內可以見到很多鳥和蝴蝶。

Hiking in the forest brings us close to the nature.
在森林裡健行可以讓我們接近大自然。

B 常說的話

Thank you for taking me here to see life on a ranch.
謝謝你帶我來看看牧場生活。

Let me feed the cows on the open pasture.
我來餵一餵這片廣大牧草上的牛。

Their dairy products taste so fresh and nutritious.
他們的乳製品嚐起來真是新鮮又有營養。

The milk comes straight from the cows on the ranch.
這牛奶是直接來自牧場的牛。

Look at the ostriches walking among the cows.
看看這些在牛群中行走的鴕鳥。

Our hiking took us to the well-designed suspension bridge.
健行後,我們來到了一座設計良好的吊橋。

In this forest area, bird-watching has a special meaning for me.
在這森林區內,賞鳥對我有種特別意義。

This place truly lives up to the name of Butterfly Valley.
這地方稱為蝴蝶谷真是名符其實。

Unit 6 Zhiben Hot Spring
知本溫泉

The quality of Zhiben Hot Spring is first-rate.
知本溫泉的水質是最上等的。

情境對話 1

A What do you think of Zhiben Hot Spring?
你覺得知本溫泉如何？

B I don't know why, but it doesn't smell at all.
不知為什麼，這（泉水）沒有任何味道。

A The spring water of Zhiben Hot Spring is odorless.
知本溫泉的泉水是沒味道。

B And the water looks so clear.
還有這水看來好清澈。

A The spring water of Zhiben Hot Spring is first-rate.
知本溫泉的泉水是一流的。

B We should come here as often as we can.
我們應該盡可能常來這裡。

情境對話 2

Ⓐ Let's order something now that we've finished bathing in the hot spring.
既然我們已經泡完溫泉,該來點些食物了。

Ⓑ I saw the advertisements of indigenous cuisine at this hotel.
我看見旅館內有原住民餐點的廣告。

Ⓐ Their dishes mostly are fresh vegetables and the meat they hunted.
他們的餐點大多是新鮮蔬菜和他們所獵到的肉類。

Ⓑ Their country dishes sound just like what I'd like to eat now.
他們的鄉村野味聽來正是我現在想吃的食物。

Ⓐ Maybe we can order a soup of bamboo sprouts to share.
或許我們可以點一碗竹筍湯來分享。

Ⓑ After the hot spring, I'm ready to enjoy this fantastic dinner.
泡完溫泉後,我準備好要來享用這頓美味的晚餐。

Ⓐ In the end, we can have some sugar apple from Taitung.
結束後我們可以吃台東的釋迦。

Ⓑ It sounds like a heavenly dinner.
聽起來像是頓十分美好的晚餐。

Ⓐ常說的話●

Zhiben Hot Spring is called the "Number One View in Eastern Taiwan".
知本溫泉有「東台灣第一景」之稱。

Zhiben Hot Spring is colorless and odorless and of high quality.
知本溫泉無色無味,水質極佳。

The temperature of Zhiben Hot Spring reaches more than 100 degrees Celsius.
知本溫泉的溫度超過攝氏一百度。

Zhiben is divided into the inner and outer hot spring areas.
知本溫泉分為內外溫泉區。

The inner hot spring area was developed later but became more prosperous.
內溫泉區較晚開發,但是變得較繁榮。

The inner and outer hot spring areas expanded and joined together.
內外溫泉區擴展開來,並且合併起來。

Indigenous people gather here and provide their country dishes.
原住民聚在這裡,提供他們的鄉村野味。

The fruits of eastern Taiwan, like sugar apple and pineapple, are offered here.
這裡提供有東台灣的水果,像是釋迦和鳳梨。

track 跨頁共同導讀 091

Ⓑ常說的話

What makes the water of Zhiben Hot Spring special?
知本溫泉的泉水有什麼特別的？

I never experience hot spring that is colorless and odorless.
我從來沒體驗過無色無味的溫泉水。

The beautiful scenery makes Zhiben Hot Spring very special.
美麗的景色使得知本溫泉非常特殊。

With so many guests here, a quiet hot spring hotel is hard to find.
這麼多的遊客在這裡，要找一家安靜的溫泉旅館很難。

I prefer a small and quiet inn where we can enjoy hot spring.
我比較喜歡小而安靜的旅社，讓我們能在那裡享受溫泉。

Let's order indigenous cuisine at this hot spring hotel.
我們來點這家溫泉旅館的原住民餐點吧。

Is sugar apple a special fruit from this region?
釋迦是這個地區的水果特產嗎？

Zhiben Hot Spring is truly a health resort.
知本溫泉真是個健康渡假村。

Unit 7　Sanxiantai
三仙台

"Sanxiantan" means Terrace of the Three Immortals.
「三仙台」的意思是三位仙人所到過的平台。

●情境對話 1●

A Look at the three giant rocks over there!
你看那邊的三塊巨石！

B How did the three rocks make their way to the island?
那三塊巨石是怎樣到那島上的？

A Legend has it that three Immortals left their footprints there.
傳說中有三位仙人在那裡留下了足印。

B Do you mean those three huge rocks are their footprints?
你是說那三塊巨石是他們的足印？

A That's what the local legend says.
當地傳說是這樣說的。

B I wonder why they chose this place.
我很好奇他們為什麼選上這個地方。

情境對話 2

A Let's walk across that eight-arch footbridge.
我們去過那座八拱步道橋吧。

B Is the bridge designed in the shape of curvy waves?
這橋是否設計為波浪造形?

A Yes, and it is one of the most famous landmarks of the east.
對,而且這是東部最有名的地標之一。

B From this bridge, I can take many good photos of Sanxiantai.
我從這橋上可以拍很多張三仙台的好相片。

A There are lots of unusual rock formations on the island waiting for you.
在島上有好多的不尋常岩石地形等著你。

B I think I see colorful coral reefs around the coasts.
我想我看見了岸邊色彩繽紛的珊瑚礁了。

A That's very likely because Sanxiantai has rich undersea natural lives.
這很可能,因為三仙台的海底生態很豐富。

B I can't believe that such a small island has so much to offer.
我真不敢相信這麼小的島嶼能提供這麼多的寶藏。

Ⓐ 常說的話

The legend of Sanxiantai makes this place even more fascinating.
三仙台的傳說使得這地方更迷人。

Three immortals left their footprints, which formed three giant rocks.
三位仙人留下了他們的足印,變成了三塊巨石。

Special rock formations can be found everywhere on the island.
在島上到處能看到特別的岩石地形。

Sanxiantai can only be reached by crossing an eight-arch footbridge.
要到三仙台,一定要經過一座八拱步道橋。

Ⓑ 常說的話

These three giant rocks can only be moved by the immortals.
這三塊巨石只有仙人搬得動。

Can I take a photo of Sanxiantai at sunset later on?
等一會兒我可以拍張夕陽下的三仙台嗎?

The natural plants on the island are very special, too.
島上的天然植物也很特別。

Chapter 7

Offshore Islands
離島

Unit 1 Introduction to Orchid Island
介紹蘭嶼

Orchid Island is an island southeast of Taiwan.
蘭嶼是台灣東南方的島嶼。

情境對話 1

A Would you like to visit Orchid Island?
你想要到蘭嶼玩嗎?

B Where is this Island?
這個島嶼在哪裡呢?

A Orchid Island is an island southeast of Taitung.
蘭嶼是台東東南方的島嶼。

B Do we have to take a small airplane to fly there?
我們要搭小飛機到那裡嗎?

A The other way to get there is to take a boat trip.
不然我們得搭船。

B I guess there is no easy way to get there.
我猜要到那裡一趟不容易。

情境對話 2

A Do you know anything about Orchid Island?
你聽過蘭嶼島嗎?

B Is it one of the islands that surround Taiwan?
那是台灣周圍的一個島嶼嗎?

A Yes, it is on the sea, southeast of Taitung County.
對,是在海上,台東縣東南方。

B Who are the residents on that island?
誰住在島上呢?

A The indigenous people living there are the Tao people.
達悟族是住在那裡的原住民。

B Are most of them fishermen?
他們大多是漁民嗎?

A Yes, they have their own traditional canoes and Flying Fish Festival.
對,他們有自己的拼板舟和飛魚祭。

B What you said makes me really want to visit Orchid Island.
你這樣說讓我真想要去蘭嶼玩。

❹常說的話

Orchid Island is formed by an undersea volcano.
蘭嶼是由海底火山形成的。

Orchid Island is also known as Redhead Island.
蘭嶼也被稱為紅頭嶼。

Summer is generally the good season to visit Orchid Island.
夏天通常是到蘭嶼玩的好季節。

You can go to Orchid Island either by boat or by airplane.
你可以坐船或搭飛機到蘭嶼。

Orchid Island is an ideal place for water sports.
蘭嶼是從事水上運動的理想地方。

Orchid Island was originally inhabited by the Tao people.
最先住在蘭嶼的是達悟族。

The Tao people are also recognized as the Yami people.
達悟族也被稱為雅美族。

Almost all Tao people rely on fishing for their livelihood.
幾乎所有達悟族人都靠捕魚為生。

Ⓑ常說的話

When is the best season to visit Orchid Island?
什麼季節到蘭嶼玩最好？

Are there many beautiful orchid flowers on the island?
在島上有很多美麗的蘭花嗎？

Are the flights canceled often because of bad weather?
航班是否會經常因為天候不佳而取消？

Do most people ride scooters on Orchid Island?
在蘭嶼大部分人都騎機車嗎？

Are there many foreigners living on the Island?
有很多外國人住在島上嗎？

Are there beautiful coral reefs around Orchid Island?
在蘭嶼周圍有美麗的珊瑚礁嗎？

Can I go snorkeling or diving around Orchid Island?
我可以在蘭嶼周圍浮潛或潛水嗎？

Do they have good doctors for emergencies?
發生意外狀況時他們有好的醫生嗎？

Unit 2 A Tour on Orchid Island
參觀蘭嶼

096 track

You get the tropical feeling on Orchid Island.
到蘭嶼可感受到在熱帶的感覺。

● 情境對話 1 ●

Ⓐ How do you feel after the boat trip?
下了船後你感覺如何？

Ⓑ Next time I will fly here.
下次我會搭飛機來這裡。

Ⓐ Have you planned anything to do here?
你計畫要在這裡做些什麼？

Ⓑ First, I'd like to sit and rest for a while.
首先，我要坐下來休息一下。

Ⓐ There is this family run café, not far from here.
有間家庭式咖啡屋，離這裡不遠。

Ⓑ That sounds like what I need now.
聽來正是我現在需要的。

track 跨頁共同導讀 096

●情境對話2●

A After the rough flight, we finally arrived in Orchid Island.
經過顛簸的飛行後,我們總算到達了蘭嶼。

B What do you think we should start with first?
你覺得我們該先做什麼?

A It all depends on what you want to see here.
這完全依你在這裡想看的事物而定。

B In my guidebook, it says the Tao people live on this island.
我的導遊書說,達悟族住在這座島上。

A In fact, it is my first visit here, too.
事實上,我也是第一次來到這地方。

B Is it possible to hire a local guide to show us around?
我們能請一位當地導遊帶我們參觀嗎?

A That sounds like a good idea.
很好的主意。

B The last thing we want is to miss whatever we must see here.
我們可不想要錯過任何在這裡該參觀的。

ⓐ常說的話

Most restaurants here offer steamed fish with rice.
這裡大部分的餐廳提供蒸魚配飯。

You can go snorkeling around Orchid Island.
你可以在蘭嶼島附近浮潛。

The corals here are in good condition.
這裡的珊瑚狀況很好。

Don't take corals or other things from the sea.
不要帶走珊瑚或海裡其它東西。

You can go swimming at the sand beaches.
你可以在沙灘游泳。

Do not throw away garbage anywhere on Orchid Island.
不要在蘭嶼任何地方亂丟垃圾。

Orchid Island has the tropical flavor.
蘭嶼有熱帶風情。

Talking to locals is a good way to get to know this place.
和當地人交談是了解這地方的好方法。

跟老外介紹台灣這本全包了

track 跨頁共同導讀 097

Ⓑ 常說的話

If I went to Orchid Island in winter, would it be less expensive?
要是我冬天去蘭嶼,費用會較低嗎?

What would you suggest me to do on Orchid Island?
你會建議我在蘭嶼做什麼?

Snorkeling around corals is the first thing I'll do here.
我首先會去這裡的珊瑚附近浮潛。

The corals around Orchid Island are incredibly beautiful.
蘭嶼附近的珊瑚不是普通的美麗。

Can I take a look at the underground houses over there?
我可以看看那邊的地下屋嗎?

Look at the colorful canoes they are making!
你看他們正在製作的彩色獨木舟!

The two men there only wear narrow loincloths.
那兩個男人只穿著丁字褲。

I doubt anyone on Orchid Island can speak English.
蘭嶼應該不會有人會說英語。

Unit 3
Indigenous People: the Tao tribe
原住民：達悟族

Orchid Island is home to the Tao people.
蘭嶼是達悟族的故鄉。

● 情境對話 1 ●

A The Tao people live on Orchid Island.
達悟族住在蘭嶼。

B What do they do to make a living?
他們靠什麼維生？

A They fish and grow millet and taro.
他們捕魚，也種小米和芋頭。

B Their lifestyle and culture are very unique.
他們的生活方式和文化很獨特。

A So far not many tourists travel here.
至今沒有很多遊客來這裡旅遊。

B Maybe it is good that way.
或許那樣很好。

情境對話 2

A Have you been to any indigenous community?
你到過任何的原住民社區嗎？

B This is my first time to be a guest in such a place.
這是我第一次到這樣的地方作客。

A We are lucky to come at a good time to see the Flying Fish Festival.
我們很幸運對的時間來，可以看飛魚祭。

B They seem to be drying the flying fish in the air.
他們似乎在曬飛魚。

A The fish is air dried and salted and then stored after being caught.
捕到魚後，他們會把魚曬乾，醃好後，加以儲藏。

B What is so special about their fishing culture?
他們的捕魚文化有什麼特別的？

A They have many customs and taboos about hunting the flying fish.
他們有很多關於捕飛魚的習俗和禁忌。

B I've never heard something like that before.
我還是第一次聽到這樣的事。

❹常說的話

The Tao people were known as the Yami people in the past.
達悟族從前被稱為雅美族。

The Flying Fish Festival is held yearly from March to June.
飛魚祭在每年的三到六月舉行。

Some fish may only be eaten by men, and some fish may not be eaten by women.
有些魚只有男人能吃,有些魚女人不能吃。

There are names for about 450 species of fish in the Tao language.
達悟族語約有 450 種魚類的名稱。

They perform a special ceremony to launch a new canoe.
新的拼板舟下水前會舉行船祭。

Many young Tao people can't speak their native language.
現在很多年輕的達悟族人不會說他們的母語。

The Tao language is different from other indigenous languages of Taiwan.
達悟族語和台灣的其它原住民族的語言不同。

The location of Orchid Island helps the preservation of their culture.
蘭嶼的位置對於他們文化的保存有助益。

track 跨頁共同導讀 099

Ⓑ常說的話

Can I see the celebration of the launch of a new canoe?
我可以觀看新的拼板舟下水前的船祭嗎?

I guess fishing is very important for the young Tao men to learn.
我猜學捕魚對達悟族的年輕男人很重要。

Is there any chance to see a master carve the canoe?
有機會觀看師傅雕刻拼板舟嗎?

Their underground houses are good against typhoons.
他們的地下屋對防颱很有用。

Hair Dance of the Tao women is very impressive.
達悟族女人的長髮舞令人印象非常深刻。

Shall we look for the pretty orchid flowers on the island?
我們去尋找島上美麗的蘭花吧。

Can we take part in the dancing in the Harvest Festival?
我們能夠加入豐年祭的舞蹈嗎?

It would be a shame if the Tao culture disappears.
要是達悟族文化消失的話,那就太可惜了。

Unit 4 Green Island
綠島

Green Island is good for scuba diving.
綠島是潛水的好地方。

●情境對話1

A Welcome to Green Island.
歡迎來到綠島。

B It looks like a tropical paradise.
看起來像是個熱帶樂園。

A Political prisoners used to be kept here.
這裡曾經關過政治犯。

B Can we visit the prisons now?
我們現在能參觀這些監獄嗎？

A Yes, the prisons are now opened for visit.
可以，這些監獄現在開放給大眾參觀。

B Let's check out what prisons were like.
我們去看看那時的監獄是什麼樣子吧。

track 跨頁共同導讀 100

情境對話 2

A We have finally made it to Green Island.
經過辛苦跋涉後,我們總算抵達了綠島。

B Was the island the old place to keep political prisoners?
這個島就是從前關政治犯的地方嗎?

A Now most people come here for scuba diving and snorkeling.
現在大部分人來這裡潛水和浮潛。

B So it has changed from an island for prisoners to a water sports resort.
所以説是由犯人島變為水上運動渡假景點了。

A You can also enjoy hot springs here.
還有溫泉可享受。

B It seems to be quite crowded with tourists here.
這裡似乎擠滿了遊客。

A We are not the only ones who want to spend their holidays here.
我們不是唯一想要在這裡度假的人。

B It shows Green Island is a good place to visit.
這表示綠島是個旅遊的好地方。

❹常說的話

Green Island was once where political prisoners were kept.
綠島曾經是關政治犯的地方。

The prisons are now open to the public.
現在監獄對外開放。

Green Island is the heaven for scuba diving and snorkeling.
綠島是潛水和浮潛的天堂。

Corals and fish are unusually beautiful around Green Island.
綠島周圍的珊瑚和魚類都異常美麗。

Green Island is very often crowded with tourists.
綠島經常擠滿了遊客。

In winter Green Island is less crowded and better for hiking.
冬天時綠島較不擁擠,較適合健行。

Some hostels on Green Island are very charming.
有些綠島的民宿很可愛。

We can cruise around Green Island if you want to.
你願意的話,我們可以搭船繞綠島一圈。

Ⓑ 常說的話

The conditions of the prisons here were awful.
那時這裡的監獄狀況很糟糕。

You must try snorkeling with me here.
你一定要和我一起試試浮潛。

Why don't you take a course of scuba diving here?
你何不在這裡上潛水的課程?

The sea life around Green Island is very rich.
綠島的海洋生態非常豐富。

I should have brought my underwater camera with me.
早知道我就帶我的潛水攝影機來了。

Let's take this cruise to go on the Pacific Ocean.
我們一起坐船去太平洋看看。

Come to the cruise ship deck with me!
和我一起來船上的甲板吧。

Watching the waves on the deck is fun.
在甲板上看浪很好玩。

Unit 5 Matzu
馬祖

Kaoliang Liquor is the specialty of Matzu.
高粱酒是馬祖的特產。

●情境對話 1●

A What do you think of the 88 Tunnel?
你覺得八八坑道怎麼樣？

B They say it is big enough to store tanks.
聽說大到可以停放坦克車。

A Now the tunnel is a winery.
現在這個坑道用來當酒窖。

B I can smell Kaoliang Liquor in the air everywhere.
空氣中到處聞得到高粱酒味。

A Many tourists come to Matzu just for Kaoliang Liquor.
很多遊客來馬祖就是為了高粱酒。

B I feel a bit drunk by just smelling it.
我光是聞到就感到有點醉了。

情境對話 2

A How about taking a short trip to Nangan Island?
我們去南竿島小遊一下如何？

B Are we going there by boat?
我們要搭船到那裡嗎？

A Yes, boat is the main transportation between the Matzu islands.
對，馬祖列島間的交通主要是靠船。

B What scenic spots can we visit on Nangan Island?
在南竿島上有什麼景點可參觀的呢？

A The 88 Tunnel over there is a must see in Matzu.
那裡的八八坑道是馬祖必遊之地。

B What else can we do on Nangan Island?
除此之外，在南竿島上還可做什麼呢？

A We can watch sunrise together at Wangniushan.
我們可以一起在望牛山看日出。

B That sounds like a perfect way to start a new day.
聽起來，那是展開嶄新一天最棒的方式。

Ⓐ 常說的話

Matzu was originally named after the sea goddess Mazu.
馬祖原先是依海神媽祖而命名的。

In fact, Matzu is composed of a group of islets.
事實上,馬祖是由一群列島所組成的。

The 88 Tunnel is now used to store Kaoliang Liquor.
八八坑道現在成為儲藏高梁酒的酒窖。

The Iron Fort shows what it was like during wartime.
在鐵堡可看出戰時情況是怎樣的。

Several scenic spots in Matzu were military bases.
許多馬祖的景點曾經是軍事要地。

You can taste all of the Matzu pastries before you buy.
所有馬祖的糕餅在買之前你都可以試吃。

Do you like to watch birds migrating through Matzu?
你喜歡觀看在馬祖過境的候鳥嗎?

Matzu has many protective areas of rare birds.
馬祖有很多稀有鳥類保護區。

跟老外介紹台灣這本全包了

track 跨頁共同導讀 103

Ⓑ常說的話

The life of soldiers in Matzu must have been very tough.
從前馬祖軍人的生活一定很辛苦。

Were any battles fought here in Matzu?
有任何戰役是在馬祖這裡開打的嗎?

Can you show me where the Mazu temple is?
你能告訴我媽祖廟在哪裡嗎?

Is it a good season now to watch migratory birds?
現在是看候鳥的好季節嗎?

The stone houses in Matzu look very strong.
馬祖的石屋看來非常堅固。

The rock formations are formed by sea water.
這些岩石地形是海水造成的。

Just tasting these pastries made me full already.
光是試吃這些糕餅我就已經飽了。

Let's rent a bike and cycle around the island!
我們來租自行車環島一圈!

Unit 6 Kinmen
金門

You will enjoy the rich culture of Kinmen.
你會喜歡金門豐富的文化。

情境對話 1

A Take a look at "the Spirit Lion Statue".
你看看這個「風獅爺」。

B What are the purposes of "the Spirit Lion Statue"?
「風獅爺」有什麼作用？

A First of all, to cease the wind.
第一個用途是鎮風。

B What else does "the Spirit Lion Statue" do?
「風獅爺」還有什麼其它作用？

A It also fights against evil spirit and prays for blessings.
還能驅邪招福。

B What an amazing angel!
真是神奇的天使！

情境對話 2

A The Kinmen Knife is the specialty in Kinmen.
金門菜刀是金門的特產。

B What makes the Kinmen Knife so special?
金門菜刀為什麼這麼特別?

A These knives are made from the bomb shells fired to Kinmen.
這些菜刀是由砲擊金門的砲彈彈殼所製成的。

B Can I pick the bomb shell here?
我可以在這裡挑選砲彈彈殼嗎?

A Yes, then the blacksmith can produce the knife for you.
可以,然後刀匠會為你製作成菜刀。

B That's something you'll never find somewhere else.
這是在其它地方所找不到的。

A Many people like to purchase the Kinmen Knife as souvenirs.
很多人喜歡買金門菜刀當紀念品。

B Of course, I'll buy one to take home, too.
當然我也會買一把帶回家。

TAIWAN Let's Go!

105 track

ⓐ常說的話●

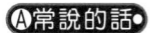

In the past, Kinmen was an important military base.
金門從前是軍事重要基地。

Kinmen is now a popular tourist destination.
金門現在是受歡迎的旅遊目的地。

Kinmen Peanut Candy is a well-known Kinmen specialty.
金門貢糖是金門出名的特產。

Come here to taste Kinmen Kaoliang Liquor!
來這裡喝喝看金門高粱酒吧。

Why not have a knife made by the blacksmith there?
何不請那裡的刀匠為你製作一把菜刀?

See that "Spirit Lion Statue" standing at the gap of the wall!
你看那站在牆縫的「風獅爺」!

Some "the Spirit Lion Statues" stand on the roofs.
有些「風獅爺」站在屋頂上。

The style of Kinmen architecture is mainly Fujianese.
金門的建築大多是福建風格。

Ⓑ 常說的話

Call a taxi for me if I get drunk from Kinmen Kaoliang Liquor.
要是我喝金門高粱酒醉了,替我叫輛計程車。

I'm afraid the Kinmen Knife will run out in the near future.
金門菜刀恐怕很快就會停售了。

I like the elegant roofs of the old houses in Kinmen.
我喜歡金門老屋古雅的屋頂。

Let's hope "the Spirit Lion Statue" can really bring good fortune.
希望「風獅爺」真能帶來好運。

With my budget, I can only buy Kinmen Peanut Candy as souvenir.
我的預算只能買金門貢糖當紀念品。

It's hard to imagine that Kinmen used to be a military base.
真難想像金門曾經是個軍事基地。

Kinmen has become a popular weekend getaway for many tourists.
金門成了很多遊客周末喜歡去的旅遊目的地。

Let's go to the beach to get away from the tourists!
我們到海灘去玩,遠離觀光客吧!

Unit 7

Penghu
澎湖

Penghu has great white sand beaches.
澎湖有絕佳的白沙灘。

●情境對話 1

A Let's play volleyball on that white sand beach!
我們去那個白沙灘上玩排球！

B That's what I was going to say.
我正要這麼說。

A Maybe we should put on sunblock lotion first.
或許我們該先擦防曬油。

B That's a good idea.
這主意不錯。

A Do you want to go swimming later?
你等一下想要游泳嗎？

B After the game we'll both lie down and rest at the beach.
玩完排球後，我們都會在沙灘上躺下來休息。

跟老外介紹台灣這本全包了

track 跨頁共同導讀 106

●情境對話2●

A What do you think of the coastal scenes of Penghu?
你覺得澎湖海岸邊的風景如何?

B They are unique and full of natural beauty.
非常獨特,充滿自然之美。

A The sea resources are so rich.
海洋資源如此豐富。

B See the turtles swimming in the waves!
你看那些在海浪中游泳的海龜!

A The coral reefs are not spoiled by people at all.
珊瑚礁一點也沒有受到人類破壞。

B The sunshine on Penghu is gorgeous.
澎湖的陽光真美。

A I think I'll sit here at the beach and watch the sunset.
我想要坐在沙灘這兒看夕陽。

B Wouldn't it be great if life could be so casual every day?
要是生活每天都這麼悠閒該有多好?

Ⓐ 常說的話

Many people buy these stones with pretty streaks on Penghu.
很多人在澎湖買紋路美麗的文石。

There are abundant geological features in the sea recreation area.
在海洋休閒區有豐富的地質風貌。

Let's take a look at the traditional fishing village here.
我們去看看這裡的傳統漁村。

Many stone houses are still in their original shapes.
很多的石屋仍然保持原貌。

Ⓑ 常說的話

People say the coastal scenes of Penghu are worth seeing.
聽說澎湖的海岸風景值得一看。

The scenery on Penghu cannot be found somewhere else.
澎湖的風景在別處找不到。

Thank you for showing me the ocean view here.
謝謝你帶我來這裡看海景。

Chapter 8

Night Markets
夜市

Unit 1

Introduction to Shilin Night Market
介紹士林夜市

Let's visit the new Shilin Night Market.
我們一起去參觀新的士林夜市吧。

● 情境對話 1 ●

A Shilin Night Market is the most famous night market in Taipei.
士林夜市是台北最有名的夜市。

B Can we get there easily?
到那裡很方便嗎?

A It is right next to MRT Jiantan Station.
夜市就位於捷運劍潭站附近。

B People say the delicacies there are both good and inexpensive.
聽說那裡的美食既好吃又便宜。

A I haven't been to Shilin Night Market since it moved to the new building nearby.
士林夜市搬到附近新建築物後,我還沒去過。

B Let's check it out together this evening.
我們今晚就一起去那裡看看吧。

跟老外介紹台灣這本全包了

track 跨頁共同導讀 108

●情境對話2

A Shilin Night Market is considered the largest night market in Taipei.
士林夜市被視為台北最大的夜市。

B Where about in Taipei is the huge night market?
這個大型夜市位在台北何處?

A It is situated in the north of Taipei.
在台北偏北的地方。

B Is it a night market, selling delicious Taiwanese dishes?
那是個賣台灣美食的夜市嗎?

A People go to Shilin Night Market to eat, to shop and to have fun.
人們到士林夜市去吃美食、購物和玩樂。

B Do the products there have good quality and cost little?
那裡的產品品質好又不貴嗎?

A Yes, the deals are so good that the night market is always crowded.
對,那兒東西物美價廉,所以夜市總是很擁擠。

B Let's head to Shilin Night Market now since we haven't had dinner.
既然我們還沒吃晚餐,我們現在就去士林夜市吧。

ⓐ 常說的話

Shilin Night Market started from the vendors gathering near a temple.
士林夜市起源於聚在一間廟附近的小販。

In the beginning, the students in that area were the main customers.
開始的時候,那地區的學生是主要顧客。

The vendors have low prices to attract students.
小販用很低的價錢來吸引學生。

Later on, some students became vendors at the night market, too.
後來,有的學生也變成了夜市的小販。

Shilin Night Market has gone through renovation many times.
士林夜市經過多次的改建。

The new building for various food stands is clean and bright.
新建築物很乾淨明亮,裡面有各種小吃攤。

This street of the souvenir shops is made in traditional Taiwanese style.
這一條紀念品商店街是屬於傳統台灣風格。

There is a stage for Taiwanese opera near the temple.
這間廟附近有舞台供台灣歌仔戲表演。

跟老外介紹台灣這本全包了

track 跨頁共同導讀 109

Ⓑ常說的話●

How did Shilin Night Market start in the very beginning?
士林夜市是如何開始的？

Is Shilin Night Market the oldest Night Market in Taipei?
士林夜市是台北最老的夜市嗎？

What time do the vendors start their business every day?
這些小販每天什麼時候開始營業？

What are some of the Taiwanese delicacies I must try here?
我非要嚐嚐看這裡的台灣美食有哪些？

Do you want to play the games at the night market with me?
你要和我玩夜市裡的遊戲嗎？

What did the old Shilin Night Market look like?
舊的士林夜市看起來怎麼樣？

How does the new Shilin Night Market compare to the old one?
新的士林夜市和舊的士林夜市比起來怎樣？

Did you often come to Shilin Night Market when you were a student?
你當學生的時候，經常來士林夜市嗎？

Unit 2

Shilin Night Market Food
士林夜市美食

110 track

Shilin Night Market Food has a good reputation.
士林夜市美食聲譽極佳。

● 情境對話 1 ●

A Look at so many fruit stands on the ground floor at Shilin Night Market.
你看士林夜市一樓這麼多的水果攤。

B What is this green round fruit called?
這個綠色圓形的水果叫什麼？

A It is called "guava".
叫「芭樂」。

B Look! They also have guavas that are red inside.
看！他們也有紅心芭樂。

A Would you like to try my favorite fruit drink, papaya milk?
你想喝喝看我最喜歡的木瓜汁嗎？

B Of course, I love juice made of fresh fruit.
當然，我愛喝新鮮果汁。

情境對話2

A On this floor you'll find all stands with Taiwanese delicacies.
在這層樓你會看見所有台灣美食的攤販。

B I've heard the oyster omelet tastes fantastic.
我聽説蚵仔煎很好吃。

A The oyster omelet at Shilin Night Market tastes best to me.
我覺得士林夜市的蚵仔煎最好吃。

B There are so many dishes to choose from.
有這麼多的餐點可以選。

A I would recommend the Doubled Layer Roll.
我會推薦大腸包小腸。

B Can you describe what it is to me?
你能描述一下那是怎樣的食物？

A It is sausage wrapped in glutinous rice.
就是香腸包在糯米中。

B That sounds very yummy.
聽起來好吃極了。

Ⓐ 常說的話

Each of the food stands has something special to offer.
每一個小吃攤都提供有特別的美食。

Many of the food stands here have 40 to 50 years of history.
很多這裡的小吃攤有四十到五十年的歷史。

The new Shilin Night Market is bigger and cleaner than the old one.
新的士林夜市比舊的士林夜市較大且較乾淨。

The lively atmosphere at Shilin Night Market draws many tourists.
士林夜市的熱鬧氣氛吸引了很多遊客。

Would you like to try a deep-fried scallion pancake?
你想要吃吃看油炸的蔥油餅嗎？

Their chicken steak is very famous.
他們的雞排很有名。

The shiny barbecued sausages can only be found here.
烤得發亮的香腸只在這裡有。

Nearby, there are also stands selling Stinky Tofu.
在這附近也有賣臭豆腐的小攤。

Ⓑ常說的話

Pearl milk tea can be found at every corner at Shilin Night Market.
在士林夜市的各角落都可以看到珍珠奶茶。

Of all the fantastic dishes here, I love rice with braised pork best.
在這裡所有美食中,我最喜歡滷肉飯。

Watching the food being prepared at Shilin Night Market is interesting.
觀看士林夜市美食製作過程很有意思。

Shilin Night Market draws huge crowds of foreign customers.
士林夜市吸引了眾多的外國顧客。

Taiwan is indeed the kingdom of fruit, especially tropical fruit.
台灣真是水果王國,特別是熱帶水果。

Why would anyone want to eat Stinky Tofu if it is stinky?
如果臭豆腐是臭的,為什麼有人想吃呢?

To me, Stinky Tofu really smells very stinky.
對我來說,臭豆腐真的聞起來非常臭。

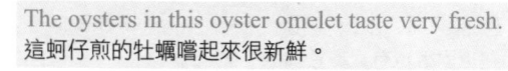

The oysters in this oyster omelet taste very fresh.
這蚵仔煎的牡蠣嚐起來很新鮮。

Unit 3

Shopping at Shilin Night Market
於士林夜市購物

Many people enjoy shopping at Shilin Night Market.
很多人喜愛到士林夜市購物。

● 情境對話 1 ●

A Are you looking for anything particular?
你在找什麼特別的東西嗎?

B I am looking for a T-shirt for my younger brother.
我在找一件給我弟弟的 T 恤。

A What sort of T-shirt are you thinking about?
你想要哪一類的 T 恤?

B He's always been into things with Chinese characters.
他總是對有中文字的東西很感興趣。

A What about that T-shirt with the Chinese character of "dragon"?
那件有中文「龍」字的 T 恤怎麼樣?

B That looks just like something he would wear.
那看起來就像是他會穿的衣服。

情境對話2

A Are you looking for toys for kids?
你在替小孩子找玩具嗎?

B Yes, my nephew would like to have some toys from Taiwan.
對,我的姪子想要一些台灣的玩具。

A Do you think he'd like to play with these puzzles?
你覺得他會喜歡玩這些拼圖嗎?

B Those puzzles you are holding look gorgeous.
你手上拿的那些拼圖看起來很漂亮。

A They are an oil painting of Jade Mountain and a water color painting of Alishan.
分別是玉山的油畫和阿里山的水彩畫。

B If my nephew doesn't like those puzzles, I'll keep them to myself.
如果我的姪子不喜歡那些拼圖,我會自己保留起來。

A They make good pictures of mountains on the wall.
可以把它們當作不錯的山景畫,掛在牆上。

B They can remind me of our time together in Taiwan, too.
同時也可以提醒我,我們在台灣一起的時光。

ⓐ常說的話

You can find all sorts of souvenirs in these shops.
在這些商店內可以找到各式各樣的紀念品。

You are sure to get your money's worth at Shilin Night Market.
在士林夜市買東西一定很劃算。

Do you need my advice about Taiwanese souvenirs?
需要我建議你可以買哪些台灣紀念品嗎?

You can find anything imaginable at Shilin Night Market.
在士林夜市你可以找到各種你想像得到的東西。

You can also find the cultural and creative products here.
在這裡你也可以看到文創產品。

Do you want to try this Chinese style shirt on?
你想要試穿一下這件中國式襯衫嗎?

Traditional blue and white bags have become popular again.
傳統藍白色的提包再度流行起來。

At Shilin Night Market, most products are sold at affordable prices.
士林夜市大部分產品的價格都很劃算。

Ⓑ常說的話

They seem to sell mostly fashion and accessories for young people.
他們似乎都在賣給年輕人的服飾。

Let's stop and take a look at these souvenir shops!
我們停下來看看這些紀念品商店吧。

They sell postcards and stamps in this souvenir shop.
這家紀念品商店有賣明信片和郵票。

I might get myself this T-shirt with the shape of Taiwan Island on it.
我大概會買這件印有台灣島的 T 恤給我自己。

Would you want to play a game with me at this stand?
你想和我一起在這一攤玩遊戲嗎?

Let me take a photo of you in front of the souvenir shop!
讓我拍一張你站在紀念品商店前的相片吧。

I really don't know which items of the accessories I should buy.
我真的不知道我該買哪幾件飾品。

My parents would love this can of Alishan Tea.
我父母親會很喜愛這罐阿里山茶。

Unit 4 Local Products
當地產品

You can find good Taiwanese products at Shilin Night Market.
你可以在士林夜市找到很好的台灣產品。

●情境對話 1

A Try a bit of this new pineapple cake!
你嚐嚐看這種新的鳳梨酥！

B It tastes like tea flavor.
嚐起來有茶的味道。

A These pineapple cakes have many different flavors.
這些鳳梨酥有很多不同的口味。

B This one tastes like cranberry.
這個嚐起來像是蔓越莓。

A All these flavors are new to me, too.
對我來說，這些也是新口味。

B I'll buy a bit of each flavor for us to taste tonight.
我每種口味都買一點，今晚我們就能都吃吃看了。

track 跨頁共同導讀 114

情境對話 2

A How did your shopping go?
你的採購進行如何？

B I saw many customers bargain with the vendors.
我看見很多客人和小販殺價。

A Some people bargain over the price, but I seldom do.
有些人會殺價，但是我很少這麼做。

B That woman paid one hundred dollars less than the original price.
那個婦人比原價少付了一百元。

A If you want to, you can bargain with the vendors.
如果你想要的話，可以和小販議價。

B I think they expect customers to bargain.
我覺得他們預料顧客會殺價。

A Maybe you are right about this.
或許你說的對。

B I think I'll buy more than one piece and then negotiate the price.
我想我會多買幾件，然後和他們議價。

Ⓐ 常說的話

Shilin Night Market is a good marketplace for many suppliers.
士林夜市是很多供應廠商的好市場。

Pearl milk tea has recently become famous Taiwanese food.
珍珠奶茶最近成了有名的台灣美食。

They sell the wine made of millet made by indigenous people.
他們有賣原住民的小米酒。

The souvenirs are designed well and cost very little.
這些紀念品設計得很好,價格很低。

Fashion products costs about one third of those in downtown Taipei.
服飾產品價格約市中心的三分之一。

Many souvenirs bear the image of Taiwan Island.
很多紀念品有台灣島的圖像。

Many handicraft works made by indigenous people are very delicate.
很多原住民所做的手工藝品非常精緻。

Now I've got all the gifts for my family and friends back home.
現在我已經買好了要給我家鄉的家人和朋友的禮物了。

track 跨頁共同導讀 115

Ⓑ常說的話

I can't believe the prices of the T-shirts in front of me!
我真不敢相信在我眼前的T恤的價錢!

It's interesting to see the clothing items lying on the ground.
看到服飾擺在地上,真有意思。

Their products are clearly targeted at the younger generation.
他們的產品很明顯是針對年輕族群的。

Some of the clothing items are from Korea and Japan.
有些服飾是來自韓國和日本。

Just hanging around the souvenir shops is a lot of fun.
光是在紀念品商店逛逛,就很好玩。

The pineapple cakes here come in so many different flavors.
這裡的鳳梨酥有很多不同的口味。

Shilin Night Market is suitable for people of all ages.
士林夜市適合所有年紀的人。

At Shilin Night Market, I get to see what the local life is like.
在士林夜市,我可以看到當地生活的風貌。

Unit 5
Guest Feedback
客人意見

116 track

How did you like Shilin Night Market?
你喜歡士林夜市嗎？

● 情境對話 1

A Did you like Shilin Night Market?
你覺得士林夜市怎麼樣？

B The food court is really like heaven to me.
美食區對我而言真的像天堂。

A Some foreign guests find it too crowded.
有些外國客人覺得太擠了。

B The night market is full of lively atmosphere.
這個夜市充滿熱鬧的氣氛。

A I enjoy going to Shilin Night Market.
我很喜歡去士林夜市。

B I'd like to visit other night markets, too.
我也想要參觀其它夜市。

track 跨頁共同導讀 116

情境對話2

A What did you buy in such a short time?
你在這麼短的時間內買了些什麼？

B Some clothes and hats and bags and so on.
一些衣服、帽子、提包等等。

A You seem to like what Shilin Night Market offers.
你似乎很喜歡士林夜市的商品。

B They have good fashion items at affordable prices.
他們有物美價廉的時尚產品。

A Are you done with your shopping?
你結束採購了嗎？

B Not really. I still haven't found a gift for my parents.
還沒。我仍未找到要給我父母的禮物。

A In that case, I'll wait for you at this coffee shop.
這樣的話，我在這間咖啡屋等你。

B And I'll head back to the night market.
那麼我回去夜市。

TAIWAN Let's Go!

❹常說的話●

Is this your first visit to a night market in Taiwan?
這是你在台灣第一次去參觀夜市嗎？

Going to night markets is part of the local life.
去夜市是當地人生活的一部分。

What do you think of Shilin Night Market?
你覺得士林夜市怎麼樣？

Is this night market similar to what you pictured?
這個夜市和你想像中的很像嗎？

Most customers can find what they want to buy here.
在這裡大部分顧客可以找到他們要買的東西。

Many products are imported from Korea and Japan.
很多產品是韓國和日本進口的。

You wouldn't want to miss Shilin Night Market.
你絕對不可錯過士林夜市。

Usually the quality of the products is reasonably good.
通常產品的品質很不錯。

track 跨頁共同導讀 117

Ⓑ常說的話

Shilin Night Market is cleaner than other night markets.
士林夜市比其它夜市乾淨。

Eating at this night market is better than in a fancy restaurant.
在這個夜市吃東西比在豪華餐廳更好。

Both food court and shopping district are very well planned.
美食區和購物區都規劃良好。

Students are not the only customers at Shinlin Night Market.
學生不是士林夜市唯一客群。

The pictures of the night market delicacies are in my guidebook.
夜市美食的照片在我的導遊書內可看到。

Do you see that group of tourists with a tour guide there?
你看到那邊的一團觀光客和一位導遊嗎？

The fashion items here are totally new to people in the States.
這些時尚產品對住在美國的人來說是全新的。

Thank you for taking me to Shilin Night Market.
謝謝你帶我來士林夜市。

Unit 6
Famous Night Markets in Taiwan.
台灣各大知名夜市

Each night market is special in its own way.
台灣各夜市都各有特色。

● 情境對話 1

A Have you been to other night markets in Taiwan?
你到過台灣其它的夜市嗎？

B No, I haven't had the chance yet.
還沒，我還沒有機會。

A Would you like to go to Huaxi Street Night Market?
你想要去華西街夜市嗎？

B Is that the famous Snake Alley?
就是那條有蛇店的名街嗎？

A Yes, and you can eat all kinds of snake delicacies there.
對，而且在那裡你可以吃到各式各樣的蛇料理。

B I think I'll pass on the snake food.
我想這個蛇類料理我就免了。

情境對話2

A Do you see all the flags flying high in the air?
你看到所有在空中飄揚的旗幟嗎?

B Yes, are they the advertisements for the food stands here?
看到了,那些是這裡小吃攤的廣告嗎?

A That's right. We are at the Tainan Flower Night Market.
對。我們來到了台南花園夜市。

B What are the most famous delicacies at this night market?
這個夜市有什麼最出名的美食?

A My favorite food here is sweet potatoes topped in hot syrup.
我最喜歡這裡的地瓜拔絲。

B What is so special about this particular dish?
這道料理有什麼特別的地方?

A Their syrup tastes really special.
他們家的糖漿嚐起來真的很特別。

B I'm going to try this dish tonight for sure.
今晚我一定要吃吃看這道料理。

Ⓐ 常說的話

Tonghua Night Market has all delicacies within walking distance.
通化夜市的美食在很短的步行距離內都可以吃得到。

The teppanyaki eatery at Tonghua Night Market is a good choice.
通化夜市的鐵板燒餐廳是個好選擇。

Herbal mutton soup is a famous dish of Yilan Luodong Night Market.
當歸羊肉湯是宜蘭羅東夜市有名的料理。

Fengjia Night Market is the most famous night market in central Taiwan.
逢甲夜市是中台灣最有名的夜市。

Ⓑ 常說的話

With so many night markets, nobody would miss out on Taiwanese delicacies.
有這麼多的夜市,應該沒有人會錯過台灣美食。

The Snake Alley looks a lot cleaner and tidier than I thought.
華西街看起來比我想的乾淨整齊多了。

Is there an official time for these night markets to close at night?
這些夜市晚上有規定結束營業的時間嗎?

Chapter 9

Temples
佛寺廟宇

Unit 1: Introduction to Fo Guang Shan
介紹佛光山

Fo Guang Shan is founded by Master Hsing Yun.
佛光山是由星雲大師所建立的。

情境對話 1

A Have you heard of "Fo Guang Shan"?
你聽過「佛光山」嗎?

B No. What does "Fo Guang Shan" mean?
不曾聽過。「佛光山」意思是?

A It means Buddha's Light Mountain.
意思是佛光普照的山。

B So, "Fo Guang Shan" must be a Buddhist center.
那麼,「佛光山」一定是個佛教中心。

A The name means spreading the Buddha's Light everywhere.
這個名字意指散播佛光到各地去。

B That's a good name.
這名字不錯。

情境對話 2

A Would you like to visit "Fo Guang Shan" with me?
你想要和我一起去「佛光山」嗎？

B What sort of place is it?
那是什麼樣的地方呢？

A It is a Buddhist Temple, founded by Master Hsing Yun in 1967.
是由星雲大師於 1967 年建立的佛寺。

B Are the people who go there all Buddhists?
去那兒的人都是佛教徒嗎？

A Not necessarily.
不一定。

B All temples with history are worth visiting.
所有富歷史性的佛寺都值得參觀。

A In that case, pack some clothes because we'll probably stay overnight.
那樣的話，收拾一下衣服，因為我們可能會在那兒過夜。

B It sounds like a "retreat" to me.
聽起來像是「閉關」。

ⓐ常說的話●

The main purpose of Fo Guang Shan is to promote Buddhism.
佛光山的主要目的是推廣佛教。

The founder of Fo Guang Shan is Master Hsing Yun, who led the construction of the temple.
佛光山的創建者是領導這個佛寺建築工程的星雲大師。

The main purpose of Buddhist colleges is to cultivate the future nuns and monks.
佛學院的主要目的是為了培育未來的比丘尼和比丘。

Lay organizations of Fo Guang Shan are very active worldwide.
佛光山的在家眾團體活躍於世界各地。

Buddhist publishing houses and art galleries are run here to promote Buddhism.
這兒還經營佛學出版社和畫廊來推廣佛教。

Their charity work includes children's homes and retirement homes.
他們的慈善工作包括育幼院和長者之家。

They use a television station as a channel to spread Buddhism.
他們用電視節目來推廣佛教。

Dialogues with other religions are encouraged in Fo Guang Shan.
佛光山鼓勵和其它宗教的對話。

B 常說的話

People who come to Fo Guang Shan often feel the ease in the air.
來到佛光山的人常能感受到空氣中自在的氣氛。

How come most people working here are females?
為什麼大部分在這裡工作的人都是女性？

How long does it take to finish the Buddhist college education?
要完成佛學院教育需要多久的時間？

Their bookstore provides a lot of Buddhist learning materials.
他們的書局有很多佛教學習材料。

Is there any way for me to meet Master Hsing Yun personally?
我可不可以和星雲大師見一次面？

The vegetarian food in the temple seems to be always good.
佛寺裡的素食似乎都很好吃。

They also run Chinese classes for foreigners like me.
他們也有開給像我這樣的外國人上的中文課。

Fo Guang Shan is a great place for Buddhists and non-Buddhists as well.
佛光山對佛教徒和非佛教徒來說，都是個好地方。

Unit 2 A Tour in Fo Guang Shan
參觀佛光山

Fo Guang Shan is a perfect place to learn about Buddhism.
佛光山是個學習佛教的最佳地方。

情境對話 1

A We are on our way to Fo Guang Shan.
我們正要前往佛光山。

B Do you think my clothes are appropriate?
你覺得我的衣著合宜嗎?

A They look all right.
看來沒問題。

B Hope the nuns over there think so, too.
希望在那兒的比丘尼也這麼認為。

A Let's go to the information counter to get some brochures.
我們去服務台取些資料。

B We'll need them because it is such a huge place.
我們會需要的,這地方真大。

track 跨頁共同導讀 122

●情境對話2●

A There comes the kind nun to greet us.
這位慈祥的比丘尼正前來迎接我們。

B Is she going to show us around Fo Guang Shan?
她會帶我們在佛光山四處參觀嗎？

A Keep your palms together to greet her like this. I'll talk to her.
像我這樣雙手合十迎接她。我來跟她說話。

B All right. Thank you.
好。謝謝。

A She wants to know if we'll stay here overnight.
她想知道我們是否要在這裡過夜。

B Why not? That's a good way to learn about Buddhism.
有何不可？在這裡過夜是學習佛教的好方法。

A I'm sure you won't be disappointed.
我相信你不會失望的。

B One question: What time do we have to get up?
我想問一下，我們幾點得起床？

Ⓐ常說的話

The main shrine is the first place people visit in Fo Guang Shan.
大殿是人們在佛光山第一個參觀的地方。

There are many other halls and shrines for people to pray at.
還有很多的大廳和大殿可讓人禮拜。

Conferences on Buddhism are often held in Fo Guang Shan.
在佛光山常舉辦佛學研討會。

The campus of Buddhist colleges is inside of Fo Guang Shan, too.
佛學院校園也位於佛光山內。

English books on Buddhism can be found in the bookstores.
在書局裡可以找到英文的佛教書籍。

Feel free to take the Buddhist pamphlets here.
你可以自由取閱這裡的佛教小冊子。

Eating in the dining hall with others is a way of spiritual practice.
在食堂和大家共同進食是修行的一種方法。

As you can see, many Buddhists wear Buddhist prayer beads on the wrist.
如你所見,很多佛教徒在手腕上戴念珠。

B 常說的話

I like the easy atmosphere of taking a walk in this huge place.
我喜歡在這偌大地方散步的輕鬆氣氛。

Do people burn incense or worship in the main shrine?
在大殿會燒香來禮拜嗎?

Should I buy some flowers to put in the front of the altar?
我該去買些花來放在佛龕前嗎?

Do they have good English books on Buddhism?
他們有優良的英文佛學書籍嗎?

Are these pretty small lucky charms for free?
這些漂亮的吉祥物是免費的嗎?

What do people wear Buddhist prayer beads for?
戴念珠是為了什麼?

Could I join the group recitation of sutra in the early morning?
我能參加一大早的早課誦經嗎?

Can I ask Buddha to fulfill my wishes when I pray to him?
在我禮佛時,能不能請求佛陀為我實現願望?

Unit 3 Buddha Memorial Center
佛陀紀念館

The world's tallest sitting Buddha statue is in front of you.
世界最高的坐佛像在你眼前。

● 情境對話 ↑

A The Fo Guang Buddha is the world's tallest sitting Buddha statue.
佛光大佛是世界最高的坐佛像。

B When was the Buddha statue completed?
佛像是什麼時候完工的呢？

A In the year of 2011, which is also 100th year of our country.
在2011年，也就是我們國家建國百年的那年。

B We are lucky to be able to see the finished Buddha statue.
我們很幸運能看到完工的佛像。

A The Fo Guang Buddha is a project totally run by Taiwanese.
佛光大佛這個建案是完全由台灣人執行的。

B It is really eye-opening to me.
真是令我大開眼界。

情境對話2

A Please follow me to the Buddha Memorial Center.
請隨我到佛陀紀念館。

B It's my pleasure.
是我的榮幸。

A Once you entered Welcoming Hall, you are on the Path to Buddhahood.
你一進入禮敬大廳,就在成佛大道上了。

B From here I can see the tall sitting Buddha statue.
從這裡我可以看見高大的坐佛像。

A The Buddha statue was designed to be able to see us from above.
依設計佛像可以從上面俯視我們。

B The giant Buddha seems to be smiling at us.
巨大的佛像似乎在對我們微笑。

A Don't miss the eight pagodas on your right and left.
不要錯過了在你左右邊的八塔。

B The Memorial Hall in front of me must be full of treasures.
在我前面的本館一定充滿了寶藏。

Ⓐ常說的話

The Buddha Memorial Center was established in 2011.
佛陀紀念館是在 2011 年建成的。

The Fo Guang Buddha faces east, with eight pagodas in the front.
佛光大佛面向東邊,前面有八座塔。

Each pagoda has its special name of Buddhist teachings.
每個寶塔的塔名都有特別的教義。

The Buddha Memorial Center is surrounded by natural scenery.
佛陀紀念館為自然風景所環繞。

Welcoming Hall greets visitors from all different places.
禮敬大廳迎接從所有不同地方來的訪客。

Thousands of Buddhist scripts are collected inside the giant Buddha statue.
大佛內收藏有無數的手抄經書。

Each place of the Memorial Hall has its special function.
本館內的每個地方都有特別的功能。

The Memorial Hall has three floors above the ground and one floor underground.
本館地上有三層樓,地下有一層樓。

跟老外介紹台灣這本全包了

track 跨頁共同導讀 125

Ⓑ 常說的話

Going through Welcoming Hall is like entering a different world.
走進禮敬大廳就好像是進入了一個不同的世界。

These pagodas along the path are designed very well.
這大道旁的寶塔設計得很好。

The sitting Buddha seems to be welcoming all visitors.
坐佛似乎在歡迎所有的來客。

It must have taken a long time to build such a huge statue of Buddha.
蓋這麼巨大的佛像一定花了很久的時間。

Can I find a good English book on Buddhism here?
我可以在這裡找到一本關於佛教的英文好書嗎?

There is an exhibition of Buddhist art that I'd like to see.
那邊有個我想看的佛教藝術展。

Would you like to see this 3D movie of Buddha's life with me?
你想和我一起看這個佛陀生平的 3D 電影嗎?

Since it is sunny, I'd like to relax in the garden with ponds.
天氣這麼好,我想在這個有水池的公園放鬆一下。

Unit 4 One Day Life in the Temple
佛門的一天

126 track

Do you know what one day life in the temple is like?
你知道佛門的一天是怎樣的嗎?

● 情境對話 1

A How about experiencing one day in the temple with me?
和我一起體驗佛門的一天如何?

B I am afraid to make lots of mistakes.
恐怕我會犯很多錯誤。.

A Don't worry about this.
這個你不用擔心。

B I hope all the nuns are very kind.
希望這裡的比丘尼都很慈祥。

A You will just have to follow what I do.
你只要跟著我做就對了。

B I guess you are right.
我猜你說的對。

track 跨頁共同導讀 126

情境對話 2

A What do you think after spending one day in the temple?
你覺得在佛堂過一天的感覺如何？

B In fact, I quite enjoyed the peaceful day.
事實上，我很享受這安靜的一天。

A What did you like best during your day there?
你最喜歡這一天的什麼？

B To be honest, the meal time is my favorite part.
老實說，我最喜歡的是用餐時間。

A What about the least favorite part?
那你最不喜歡的部分呢？

B I have to say the morning class.
我得說是早課。

A What makes you think so?
為何你這麼說？

B Can you suggest having breakfast before the morning class?
你能建議在早課前先吃早餐嗎？

Ⓐ常說的話●

In the morning, bell and drum sounds wake up all people.
清早時,鐘聲和鼓聲喚醒所有人。

The morning class is recitation of Buddhist scripts in the main hall.
早課是在大廳頌經。

Having meals with others is a way of spiritual practice, too.
和其他人一起用餐也是一種修行。

While eating, one is supposed to think about being grateful.
在用餐時要想到感恩。

During the whole dining process, we should all stay quiet.
整個用餐過程中,我們都應該要安靜。

News is usually announced during the meal time.
在用餐時間通常有消息宣布。

Labor work is part of daily routines in the temple.
出坡是佛堂的例行工作之一。

The duty of the nuns and monks is to spread Buddhist teachings.
出家人的責任就是散播佛法。

B 常說的話

Is the life in the temple very boring and tough?
佛門的一天很無聊很辛苦嗎?

Do the nuns and monks grow their own vegetables?
出家人為自己種蔬菜嗎?

What will happen if they miss the morning class?
要是他們錯過了早課,會發生什麼事?

Is the evening class exactly the same as the morning class?
晚課和早課完全相同嗎?

What do they try to achieve by reciting Buddhist scripts?
他們誦經為的是什麼?

I won't join the morning class because I can't understand Chinese.
我不參加早課了,因為我不懂中文。

The only thing I can do well in the temple is sweeping floor.
我在佛堂唯一能做得好的事就是掃地。

Eating great vegetarian meals served by others is so nice.
吃由別人服務的美味素食,真是不錯。

Unit 5 Learning Meditation
學習靜坐

Meditation can help you focus your attention.
靜坐可以幫助你專心。

●情境對話 1●

A Have you tried meditation before?
你試過靜坐嗎?

B You mean sitting still and doing nothing?
你指的是坐著什麼也不做嗎?

A It's more than that.
不是只有這樣。

B I'd like to learn how to meditate.
我想要學習如何靜坐。

A You can join this one day meditation camp.
你可以參加靜坐一日營。

B I'll give it a try.
我會試試看。

情境對話 2

A What have you learned from your meditation camp?
你在靜坐營學到了什麼?

B First of all, I learn to calm down.
首先我學會了冷靜下來。

A Could you sit still for such a long time?
你能坐這麼久都不動嗎?

B That's not a problem, but it's hard to concentrate the whole time.
那不是問題,但很難全程都專心。

A Did you learn any special techniques to help concentration?
你學了什麼幫助專心的特別技巧?

B Counting breathing helps me most.
數息對我幫助最大。

A Do you feel you can think more clearly than before?
你覺得思想比以前清晰嗎?

B I think so.
我是這麼認為。

ⓐ 常說的話●

In many religions, meditation is considered a spiritual practice.
很多宗教視靜坐為修行方式。

There are many different types of meditation.
有很多不同的靜坐類別。

To focus on what you are doing now is a way of meditation.
專心於你現在所做的事是一種禪修。

Drinking tea during the breaks of meditation sessions is refreshing.
在靜坐的休息時間喝茶很能提振精神。

Meditation can help reduce mental and physical stress.
靜坐有助於降低精神上和身體上的壓力。

Many Buddhists achieve high level of understanding by meditation.
很多佛教徒藉著靜坐達到很高的體悟。

Meditation can be practiced almost everywhere at any time.
靜坐幾乎隨時隨處都可以練習。

You can practice meditation with a group of people or alone.
你可以和一群人一起練習靜坐或是獨自練習也可以。

跟老外介紹台灣這本全包了

track 跨頁共同導讀 129

Ⓑ常說的話

Is the one day meditation camp run by a nun?
禪修一日營是由一位比丘尼帶領的嗎?

Is the instruction of meditation in English, too?
靜坐也有英文的指示嗎?

This time I can really feel the air goes into my belly and out.
這次我真能感受氣體在我的腹部進出。

Just to focus on breathing is not easy in the beginning.
剛開始要專注在呼吸上就很不容易。

Counting breathing helps me to focus my attention.
數息幫助我專心。

After twenty minutes my thoughts wandered everywhere.
二十分鐘後我思緒紛飛。

In this meditation camp I met people of different nationalities.
在這個禪修營我遇到了很多不同國籍的人。

Next time I'll try a meditation class of a higher level.
下次我會試試看更高層次的靜坐課程。

Unit 6
After the Visit to Fo Guang Shan
參觀佛光山後心得

How do you feel about your visit to Fo Guang Shan?
你覺得到佛光山參觀的感覺如何？

情境對話 1

A How do you feel after your visit to Fo Guang Shan?
參觀佛光山後你感覺如何？

B It was a very special experience.
這是一段特別的經驗。

A Was that the first time for you to visit a Buddhist temple?
是你第一次參觀佛寺嗎？

B Yes, and to me, it is like a small village.
對，對我而言像是個小村莊。

A Do you like the feeling there?
你喜歡那裡的感覺嗎？

B Very much so.
非常喜歡。

情境對話 2

A Did you enjoy your visit to Fo Guang Shan?
你喜歡佛光山嗎？

B Yes, they were all very welcoming.
很喜歡，他們都非常熱情歡迎我們。

A How did that compare to a church?
和教堂比起來如何呢？

B I've never been to a church of that size.
我所到過的教堂，規模沒有像那樣大的。

A Describe how you felt when you walked there.
描述一下，剛走進那裡時你感覺如何？

B I felt unusually calm and relaxed.
我感到不尋常的平靜和放鬆。

A Would you like to visit Fo Guang Shan again?
你會想要再來參觀佛光山嗎？

B Yes, because it feels like a spiritual refuge to me.
會，因為我覺得佛光山對我像是個精神的庇護所。

ⒶA常說的話●

Many of the people working here are volunteers.
很多人在這裡當志工。

Most of the funds for the temple come from donations.
道場大部分的基金來自於捐款。

The Fo Guang Shan temple is very well maintained.
佛光山維護得非常好。

Usually I come here to clear up my mind.
通常我來這裡洗滌我的心思。

I pray to Buddha in the main shrine immediately after I arrive here.
我一到達這裡就在大殿禮佛。

When I meditate, I often find the solution to the problems.
我常在靜坐時找到問題的解決方法。

How do you feel about the temple as a non-Buddhist?
身為非佛教徒,你覺得這個佛寺怎麼樣?

I'm glad that you managed to join our morning class.
我非常高興你能夠來參加我們的早課。

Ⓑ常說的話

Thank you so much for showing me Fo Guang Shan.
謝謝你帶我來佛光山參觀。

Please let me know if there is any meditation camp.
如果有任何的靜坐營,請通知我。

Even though I'm not a Buddhist, I like this place.
雖然我不是佛教徒,我很喜歡這地方。

The sincerity of Buddhist followers is very impressive.
佛教徒的虔誠令人印象深刻。

The main shrine of Fo Guang Shan is awesome.
佛光山的大殿很莊嚴。

Many visitors here are not Buddhists.
很多非佛教徒來這裡遊玩。

Next time I'd like to take part in a meditation class.
下次我會參加靜坐班。

Please give me the addresses of Fo Guang Shan in the States.
請給我佛光山在美國的地址。

Unit 7: Famous Buddhist Temples in Taiwan
台灣各大佛寺。

Famous Buddhist temples are all over Taiwan.
台灣各處都有知名的佛寺。

情境對話 1

A Have you been to other Buddhist temples in Taiwan?
你到過台灣其它的佛寺嗎?

B No, but now I'd like to.
沒有,但是我很想去。

A It is good for all people to visit a temple.
參觀佛寺對所有人都很好。

B Even a non-religious person like me enjoys such a visit.
即使是像我這樣沒有信仰的人也很喜歡。

A A Buddhist temple should be welcoming to all.
佛寺應該要歡迎所有人。

B Fo Guang Shan has achieved this goal.
佛光山已達到了這個目的。

情境對話 2

A Do you have questions about Buddhist temples in Taiwan?
你有什麼關於台灣佛寺的問題嗎？

B What are some other Buddhist temples in Taiwan like?
台灣其它的佛寺是怎麼樣的？

A Each school has its own strong points.
每個派別都有各自的強項。

B Can you give me some examples?
你可以給我些例子嗎？

A For example, meditation is stressed in Dharma Drum Mountain.
例如，法鼓山很強調靜坐禪修。

B What is another example?
還有其它的例子嗎？

A "Tzu Chi" is famous for charity work and hospitals.
慈濟以慈善工作和醫院聞名。

B Of course, all of them contribute a lot to the society.
當然，他們都對社會貢獻良多。

Ⓐ 常說的話

Stop by famous temples on the way while traveling in Taiwan.
當你在台灣旅遊時,有機會就停下來參觀佛寺。

The medical members of "Tzu Chi" helped much after the 921 Earthquake.
九二一大地震發生後,慈濟的醫療團隊幫了很大的忙。

Many staff members of "Tzu Chi" hospitals are Buddhists.
很多慈濟醫院的醫療人員是佛教徒。

Chung Tai Chan Monastery is the tallest temple in the world.
中台禪寺是世界最高的佛寺。

Ⓑ 常說的話

Why do people stay overnight in a Buddhist temple?
為什麼有人要在佛寺過夜?

Most Buddhist temples attract many tourists during public holidays.
大部分的佛寺在國定假日都吸引了很多遊客。

Don't the nuns and monks feel a little disturbed by tourists?
那些比丘尼和比丘不會覺得有點被遊客所打擾?

Chapter 10

Festivals
節日

Unit 1 The Lunar New Year
農曆新年

Do you know how the Lunar New Year is celebrated?
你知道農曆新年是怎樣慶祝的?

● 情境對話 1 ●

A Do you know how the Lunar New Year is celebrated?
你知道農曆新年是怎樣慶祝的?

B No, I don't. Can you tell me something about it?
我不清楚。你可以告訴我嗎?

A All families get together for dinner on Lunar New Year's Eve.
所有家庭在農曆除夕夜聚在一起吃團圓飯。

B Are there special dishes for the reunion dinner?
團圓飯有什麼特別餐點嗎?

A Yes, and each of them has a special meaning.
有的,而且每道菜都有特別意義。

B Can I join your family for the reunion dinner on the Eve?
我可以在除夕夜參加你的團圓飯嗎?

跟老外介紹台灣這本全包了

track 跨頁共同導讀 134

● 情境對話 2 ●

A You are about to experience the Lunar New Year in Taiwan.
你就將要體驗台灣的農曆新年了。

B That sounds so exciting to me.
聽起來很刺激。

A When I was a kid, I always looked forward to the Red Envelopes.
我小的時候總是很期待紅包。

B What are the Red Envelopes?
什麼是紅包?

A They are small red paper envelopes that contain money.
是裝有錢的紅色小信封。

B Do you receive the Red Envelopes as gifts?
你們收紅包當禮物?

A Only when you are a kid, but you give the Red Envelopes after you grow up.
只有在小時候,但是長大後要給紅包。

B It is much more fun to be a kid than an adult.
還是當小孩比當大人好玩。

ⓐ常說的話●

Most Taiwanese get a week holidays for the Lunar New Year.
大部分台灣人農曆新年有一星期的假。

Before the Lunar New Year's Day, all families clean up their places.
農曆新年前,所有家庭會進行大掃除。

Most people give out the Red Envelopes after the reunion dinner.
大部分人在團圓飯後發紅包。

At the Lunar New Year's Eve, people set off firecrackers.
在農曆年除夕人們會放鞭炮。

On Lunar New Year's Day, people dress in new clothes to visit their relatives.
農曆新年那一天,人們穿著新衣去拜訪親戚。

On the second day of the Lunar New Year, married daughters visit their parents with their husbands and children.
大年初二,結了婚的女兒們帶著先生和孩子去拜訪他們的父母。

Colorful dragon and lion dances are in the streets.
街上有色彩鮮豔的舞龍舞獅。

跟老外介紹台灣這本全包了

track 跨頁共同導讀 135

All people hope to start a new year with a fresh beginning.
所有人希望在新年有全新的開始。

Ⓑ常說的話

On what date is your Lunar New Year's Day?
你們農曆新年是在哪一天?

How long will the Lunar New Year holidays last in Taiwan?
台灣的農曆新年假期持續多久?

Will all the shops be closed during the Lunar New Year's holidays?
所有商店在農曆新年假期都會停止營業嗎?

Do you give the Red Envelopes to your nephews?
你會給你的姪子紅包嗎?

Can you teach me some lucky phrases in Chinese?
你可以教我一些中文的吉祥話嗎?

Is it possible for me to learn dragon and lion dances?
我可以有機會學舞龍舞獅嗎?

Why are there red signs with Chinese characters everywhere?
為什麼到處有寫滿中文字的紅條子?

Is Lunar New Year also celebrated by other peoples?
有其他國人也慶祝農曆新年嗎?

Unit 2 The Lantern Festival
元宵節

Carrying a lantern along the streets is fun.
在街上提燈籠很好玩。

情境對話 1

A How about buying a lantern for the Lantern Festival?
我們去買個元宵節的燈籠如何？

B What kinds of lanterns do you usually carry?
你通常都提什麼樣的燈籠？

A Usually I carry the animal of the year.
通常我都提當年的生肖。

B There seems to be all kinds of lanterns in this store.
在這個店裡似乎有各種的燈籠。

A You can pick any lantern you like.
你可以挑任何你喜歡的燈籠。

B I'll take this lantern of Sponge Bob.
那麼我挑這個海綿寶寶的燈籠。

跟老外介紹台灣這本全包了

track 跨頁共同導讀 136

● 情境對話 2

A Have you tasted "Tangyuan" before?
你吃過湯圓嗎?

B What is "Tangyuan"?
什麼是湯圓?

A It is a glutinous rice ball eaten at the Lantern Festival.
是元宵節所吃的一種糯米糰。

B What else do you do during the festival?
除此之外,節慶期間還有什麼活動?

A People carry lanterns or watch lantern parades.
人們提燈籠或看燈會。

B Do families get together at this time?
這個時候所有家人團聚在一起嗎?

A Many families get together and enjoy guessing lantern riddles.
很多家庭團聚在一起,享受猜燈謎。

B I am sure they eat "Tangyuan" at the same time.
想必這個時候他們在吃湯圓。

ⓐ常說的話

People enjoy a family reunion on the night of the Lantern Festival.
元宵夜時人們享受家庭團圓。

Traditionally, the Lantern Festival is the last day of the Lunar New Year.
傳統上來說,元宵節是農曆新年的最後一天。

"Tangyuan" is made of glutinous rice balls with fillings, cooked in a soup.
湯圓是包有內餡的糯米糰,並在湯中烹調。

"Tangyuan" has different fillings, such as peanut butter and sesame.
湯圓有不同的內餡,像是花生醬和芝麻。

Every child brought up here has experienced carrying a lantern.
所有在這裡長大的小孩都有提燈籠的經驗。

You can learn to make a lantern at the community center.
你可以在社區中心學習如何做燈籠。

In the Tang Dynasty, guessing lantern riddles became part of the festival.
在唐朝猜燈謎成為節慶的一部分。

The lantern riddles are often about health and family prosperity.
元宵燈謎通常和健康及家族興隆相關。

跟老外介紹台灣這本全包了

track 跨頁共同導讀 137

Ⓑ常說的話

Can you show me how to make a lantern?
你可以教我如何做燈籠嗎?

The paper lantern looks very pretty, but is it safe?
紙燈籠看起來很美,但是安全嗎?

The calligraphy on the surface of that lantern is very elegant.
那個燈籠上的書法很優美。

Please take me to watch a lantern parade in Taipei.
請帶我去看台北燈會。

How amazing the glowing dragon lantern in the parade is!
遊行中發光的龍型燈籠真是驚人!

If I could make "Tangyuan" by myself, I'd be very happy.
要是我自己會做湯圓,我會很開心

"Tangyuan" with sesame filling is the best I've tasted so far.
芝麻餡的湯圓是目前我吃過最好吃的湯圓。

I wouldn't be able to understand the lantern riddles at all.
我完全沒辦法了解燈謎。

Unit 3 Tomb Sweeping Day
清明節

Tomb Sweeping Day is a day to worship ancestors.
清明節是祭拜祖先的日子。

情境對話 1

A In a few days it will be Tomb Sweeping Day.
再過幾天就是清明節。

B What activities do you do on that day?
那天你們有什麼活動？

A We clean up the weeds around the ancestors' tombs.
我們整理祖先墳墓邊的雜草。

B Do you clean up the tombs together with other family members?
你們和其他家族成員一起清理墳墓嗎？

A That's right, and it is a day for family reunion, too.
對，那天也是家族團圓的日子。

B That sounds like a good tradition.
聽起來這個傳統很好。

情境對話 2

A I'm going to buy some spirit money for Tomb Sweeping Day.
我要去買點清明節用的紙錢。

B Is it the paper money you burn to offer to the ancestors?
就是你們為祖先所燒的紙錢嗎？

A You're right, and we burn it next to the tombs.
你說的對，而且我們在墳墓邊燒紙錢。

B Westerners don't usually worship their ancestors like that.
西方人通常不會像這樣祭拜祖先。

A We also lay food out in front of the tombs with smoking incense.
我們還在墳墓前擺上食物，還點上香。

B Do all family members get together for that ceremony?
所有家族成員都會聚在一起祭拜嗎？

A Some families send their representatives.
有的家庭派他們的代表來參加。

B In comparison, ancestors in the west might get more neglected.
相較起來，西方的祖先可能比較受忽略。

ⒶTomb 常說的話●

Tomb Sweeping Day is on April 5th and is a national holiday.
清明節在四月五日,是個國定假日。

Offerings are laid out for the ancestors, along with spirit money.
給祖先的祭品會和紙錢一起擺放。

Some cold dishes are eaten especially on Tomb Sweeping Day.
清明節時會吃某些特別的冷食。

It is a good tradition to clean up the graves of ancestors.
清掃祖先的墳墓是個優良傳統。

People celebrate the coming of spring on Tomb Sweeping Day, too.
人們在清明節也慶祝春天的來臨。

Afterwards we eat the food we offered to our ancestors.
之後我們食用我們給祖先的祭品。

Incense burning is very important in the ceremony.
燒香在祭拜儀式中很重要。

Spirit money is paper money we burn for our ancestors in another world.
紙錢是用紙做的錢,我們燒紙錢是為了給在另一個世界的祖先。

B 常說的話

Is Tomb Sweeping Day a national holiday?
清明節是一個國定假日嗎?

Are the tombs of your ancestors in Taiwan or in China?
你祖先的墳墓是在台灣還是在中國?

What are some of the dishes you offer to your ancestors?
你會準備哪些祭品給祖先?

Do you think your ancestors could receive the spirit money?
你想你的祖先收得到紙錢嗎?

Can you hire people to maintain the tombs of your ancestors?
能夠雇人來維護你的祖先的墳墓嗎?

Do you really think your ancestors can affect you?
你真的認為你的祖先能影響你嗎?

Tomb sweeping is a good tradition to keep.
清明節是個值得保留的優良傳統。

Do you take part in the ceremony on Tomb Sweeping Day?
你會參加清明節的祭祖儀式嗎?

Unit 4 The Dragon Boat Festival
端午節

Take a look at the dragon boat racing over there!
你看那邊的龍舟賽!

●情境對話 1●

A Do you see those colorful dragon boats?
你看到那些色彩鮮豔的龍舟了嗎?

B Are they racing now?
現在它們在比賽嗎?

A Yes, it's for the Dragon Boat Festival.
對,是為了端午節。

B Really? That sounds quite interesting.
真的?聽起來非常有意思。

A The yellow dragon boat just got the first prize.
那艘黃色的龍舟剛得到第一名。

B Let me quickly take a photo.
讓我快拍張照片。

情境對話 2

A Do you want to watch the dragon boat racing?
你想要看龍舟競賽嗎?

B Of course, please take me with you.
當然想,請帶我一起去看。

A You've heard of the Dragon Boat Festival, haven't you?
你聽過端午節吧?

B I don't think so.
我想沒有。

A It is a holiday for Qu Yuan, who drowned himself in a river.
是一個為了紀念投江自盡的屈原的假日。

B Why did he do that to himself?
他為什麼要投江自盡呢?

A The emperor at his time wouldn't listen to him.
當時的皇帝不願意聽他的話。

B I suppose it was to the emperor's loss.
我想損失的是那個皇帝。

❹常說的話

The Dragon Boat Festival is on the fifth day of the fifth lunar month.
端午節是農曆五月五日。

Qu Yuan threw himself into the Miluo River and died.
屈原投汨羅江自盡。

The locals dropped wrapped rice into the river so that fish wouldn't eat Qu Yuan's body.
當地人將包好的飯投入河裡,魚才不會去吃屈原的屍體。

Rice dumplings are sticky rice wrapped in bamboo leaves.
粽子是包在竹葉裡的米糕。

The locals paddled out on boats to look for Qu Yuan's body.
當地人划船去尋找屈原的屍體。

Nowadays people hold dragon boat races at the Dragon Boat Festival.
現在人們在端午節舉行龍舟賽。

Many people wear perfumed medicine bags to keep away evil spirit.
很多人配戴香包來避邪。

In Taiwan, the Dragon Boat Festival is also celebrated as "the Poet's Day".
在台灣,端午節也是詩人節。

B 常說的話

Do you come here to watch dragon boat races every year?
你每年都來這裡看龍舟競賽嗎？

That dragon boat over there is paddled by international athletes.
那邊是國際選手組成的龍舟隊。

Rice dumplings are my favorite Chinese food.
粽子是我最喜歡的中國食物。

Can you teach me how to wrap a rice dumpling?
你能教我包粽子嗎？

Why are those people trying to make an egg stand at noon?
為什麼那些人試著在正午的時間立蛋？

Do you hang some herbs on your door as well?
你也會在家門掛草本植物嗎？

Do you have a day off for the Dragon Boat Festival?
你們端午節有放假嗎？

I find these perfumed medicine bags so lovely and well-designed.
我覺得這些香包很可愛而且設計良好。

Unit 5 Chinese Valentine's Day
七夕情人節

Lovers exchange gifts on Chinese Valentine's Day.
情人們在七夕情人節時交換禮物。

●情境對話 1●

A What are you going to do on Chinese Valentine's Day?
你七夕情人節時要做什麼?

B Do you have a different Valentine's Day?
你們的情人節和我們的不一樣嗎?

A Chinese Valentine's Day is on the 7th of July on the lunar calendar.
七夕情人節是農曆七月七日。

B What is the origin of Chinese Valentine's Day?
七夕情人節的起源是什麼?

A It is really an old and long love story.
那真的是個古老的長篇愛情故事。

B I can't wait to hear it.
我等不及要聽這故事。

情境對話 2

A Do you know why there'll be special offers in restaurants soon?
你知道為什麼餐廳快要有特別優惠？

B Are there any holidays coming?
有什麼節日快到了嗎？

A Chinese Valentine's Day is coming, and everyone seems to be excited.
七夕情人節快到了，大家似乎都很興奮。

B Is it similar to the western Valentine's Day?
那和西洋的情人節很像嗎？

A Yes, except that people here give gifts only to their lovers.
是的，除了一點，就是這裡的人只送禮物給他們的情人。

B So it is a day exclusively for lovers.
所以這是專屬於情人的日子。

A Flower shops and restaurants love Chinese Valentine's Day.
花店和餐廳熱愛七夕情人節。

B It is not hard to understand why.
不難了解為什麼。

Ⓐ常說的話

The Cowherder and the Weaver Maid fell in love without the permission of Heaven.
牛郎和織女沒有天庭允許而陷入了愛河。

They were so in love with each other that they neglected their duties.
他們熱戀到忽略了他們的職責。

The Goddess of Heaven came down to take the Weaver Maid back.
王母娘娘下來人間要帶織女回去。

The Goddess of Heaven took off her gold hair-pin and made a stroke.
王母娘娘取下她的髮簪,劃了一道線。

The stroke formed the Milky Way and separated the Cowherder and the Weaver Maid forever.
那道線形成了銀河,將牛郎和織女永遠分開。

Thousands of magpies built a bridge for them to meet each other.
成千的喜鵲建七鵲橋,讓他們相會。

The Goddess finally agreed to allow them to see each other once a year on the 7th of July.
王母娘娘最後同意讓他們於每年的七月七日相會一次。

跟老外介紹台灣這本全包了

track 跨頁共同導讀 143

B 常說的話

Please tell me about the origin of Chinese Valentine's Day.
請告訴我七夕情人節的起源。

Didn't the Cowherder notice that the Weaver Maid was a fairy?
牛郎怎麼沒有注意到織女是仙女？

The Cowherder and the Weaver Maid shouldn't have neglected their duties.
牛郎和織女不該忽略了他們的職責。

To see each other only once in a year is a pity for a married couple.
對夫妻來說，一年只能見一次面很可憐。

The legend of the Cowherder and the Weaver Maid sounds like a sad romance.
牛郎和織女的傳奇故事，聽起來像是個悲哀的愛情故事。

Do young people here celebrate two Valentine's Days?
這裡的年輕人慶祝兩個情人節嗎？

The flower shops must make lots of money on Chinese Valentine's Day.
在七夕情人節時，花店一定賺很多錢。

Is Chinese Valentine's Day also celebrated in other Asian countries?
其它亞洲國家也慶祝七夕情人節嗎？

Unit 6 Hungry Ghost Festival
中元節

At Hungry Ghost Festival all ghosts will come out.
中元節時所有鬼魂都會出現。

情境對話 1

A We have a day for ghosts, Hungry Ghost Festival.
我們這裡有中元節,那是個鬼節。

B Is that similar to Halloween?
那和萬聖節相似嗎?

A Not quite similar.
不太相似。

B When is this Hungry Ghost Festival?
這個鬼節在哪一天?

A The 15th of July of the lunar calendar, the Ghost Month.
農曆的七月十五日,農曆七月是鬼月。

B What can I do to avoid the ghosts around that time?
在這個時候我能夠做些什麼來避開鬼魂?

跟老外介紹台灣這本全包了

track 跨頁共同導讀 144

●情境對話 2●

A Many people burn incense in front of their stores.
很多人在他們店門前燒香。

B What god are they worshiping?
他們在拜什麼神？

A Today is Hungry Ghost Festival, a day when all ghosts come out.
今天是中元節，在這天所有鬼魂都會出現。

B Are they worshiping the ghosts?
他們在拜鬼嗎？

A All people who died before us are worshiped on this day.
這天我們祭拜所有比我們早離世的人。

B Your ancestors are worshiped on Tomb Sweeping Day, aren't they?
你們在清明節時祭拜祖先，不是嗎？

A Some ghosts, who are not worshiped, wander around for food.
有些沒人拜的鬼魂四處遊蕩，尋找食物。

B Now I see what the food on the tables is for.
現在我明白桌上的食物是做什麼用的了。

Ⓐ常說的話

There are rituals for the Hungry Ghost Festival in almost all temples.
幾乎所有的佛寺廟宇都有中元節的法會。

In Buddhist temples, ancestors are especially worshiped on this day.
在佛寺內,這天是特別用來祭拜祖先的。

Food and drinks are laid out in front of doors to serve the hungry ghosts.
在門前放食物和飲料是為了要給餓鬼吃。

People worship at the Hungry Ghost Festival for peace of mind.
人們在中元節祭拜以求心安。

In the Ghost Month, many hungry ghosts wander about.
在鬼月有很多餓鬼四處遊蕩。

We hope the ghosts do not make trouble for us.
我們希望鬼魂不要給我們製造麻煩。

In the Ghost Month, many people avoid going swimming.
在鬼月很多人避免去游泳。

Many ghost stories are talked about in the Ghost Month.
在鬼月人們談論很多鬼故事。

B 常說的話

Is it a Buddhist or a Taoist festival originally?
這原先是佛教或道教的節日？

Your hungry ghosts sound like the ghosts at Halloween.
你們的餓鬼聽起來像是萬聖節的鬼魂。

Do you think that ghosts really exist?
你覺得鬼真的存在嗎？

Do you think there are good ghosts and bad ones?
你認有好鬼和壞鬼嗎？

Have you ever seen a ghost in the Ghost Month?
你曾在鬼月看見過鬼嗎？

If you saw a ghost, how would you react?
要是你看到鬼，你會做何反應？

If the ghosts were your ancestors, they would not hurt you.
要是那鬼魂是你的祖先，他們應該不會傷害你。

Do you think hungry ghosts could receive the spirit money?
你認為餓鬼收得到紙錢嗎？

Unit 7　Mid-Autumn Festival
中秋節

How about tasting the hand-made moon cake?
要吃吃看手工做的月餅嗎？

●情境對話 1●

A Do you see many stores selling moon cake now?
你看到很多店家現在正在賣月餅嗎？

B Why are they called moon cake?
為何稱為月餅？

A They are sweet pastry eaten at the Mid-Autumn Festival.
那是中秋節時所吃的甜點。

B Is it a festival about the moon?
那是個關於月亮的節日嗎？

A On that night, the moon is said to be most beautiful.
在那天晚上月亮據說是最美的。

B Let's watch the moon together on that night.
我們那天晚上一起賞月吧。

track 跨頁共同導讀 146

情境對話2

A The Mid-Autumn Festival is around the corner.
中秋節就快到了。

B When is it exactly?
究竟是哪一天呢？

A It is on August 15 of the lunar calendar, and this year it is on September 30th.
是農曆的八月十五日，今年是在國曆的九月三十日。

B What are you going to do to celebrate it?
你那天要做什麼慶祝活動？

A My family will get together and have a barbecue outdoors.
我的家人會聚在一起烤肉。

B Why do you have a barbecue at the Mid-Autumn Festival?
為什麼你們要在中秋節烤肉呢？

A My family just wants to get together to admire the moon together.
我的家人只是想要聚在一起賞月。

B Moon cake is also part of the feast, right?
月餅也同時是大餐的一部分，對吧？

Ⓐ 常說的話

The Mid-Autumn Festival is also known as the Moon Festival.
中秋節同時也稱為月節。

Chang-Er took her husband's magic medicine and flew to the moon.
嫦娥吃了她先生的仙藥,飛到月亮上去。

The Jade Rabbit pounds medicine, together with Chang-Er.
玉兔搗藥,陪伴著嫦娥。

Chang-Er and the Jade Rabbit live on the moon forever.
嫦娥和玉兔永遠住在月亮上。

Ⓑ 常說的話

Admiring the moon with the family must be a lot of fun.
和家人一起賞月一定很好玩。

Is there anywhere I can learn how to make moon cake?
有沒有可以讓我學做月餅的地方?

I like the Cantonese style moon cake best.
我最喜歡廣式月餅。

Pineapple cake is also found in the moon cake box I received.
在我收到的月餅盒內我也發現了鳳梨酥。

Chapter 11

Health Trip
健康之旅

Unit 1
Tai Chi
太極拳

Let's do Tai Chi in the morning!
早上和我們一起打太極拳!

●情境對話 1●

A Would you like to learn Tai Chi with us?
你要不要和我們一起學太極拳?

B Is it very difficult to learn?
那很難嗎?

A Not at all.
一點也不難。

B What do I have to wear?
我穿什麼好呢?

A Any large and soft clothes will do.
只要是寬鬆的衣褲就可以。

B That won't be a problem.
那沒問題。

情境對話 2

A Do you want to learn Tai Chi with us at 7:00 tomorrow morning?
明早七點你要和我們一起學太極拳嗎？

B That sounds a bit too early for me.
對我來說有點太早了。

A Early to bed and early to rise makes you healthy, wealthy and wise.
早睡早起可以讓人健康、富有以及聰明。

B Is Tai Chi worth the effort to get up so early?
太極拳值得這麼早起嗎？

A The air in the morning in the park is suitable for Tai Chi.
早晨公園內的空氣適合打太極拳。

B Is your health getting better by practicing Tai Chi?
你的健康有因練習太極拳而變好嗎？

A Absolutely.
當然有。

B Tomorrow I'll join you in the park.
明天我會到公園加入你們。

ⓐ常說的話

Tai Chi is a type of Chinese martial art.
太極拳是一種中國武術。

People practice Tai Chi for both defense and health benefits.
人們為了防禦和健康而練太極拳。

Tai Chi classes are offered in most community centers.
大部分社區中心都有提供太極拳課程。

In recent years, Tai Chi has become popular among the younger generation.
最近幾年來,太極拳在年輕一輩中漸受歡迎。

The slow movements with breathing techniques relax body and mind.
緩慢的動作加上呼吸技巧讓身心放鬆。

There are many schools for Tai Chi, and some of them have fast paces.
太極拳有很多學派,有些派別的動作快速。

There are variations in Tai Chi, such as Tai Chi with a sword or a fan.
太極有許多的變種,像是太極劍或功夫扇。

By focusing on the breathing in Tai Chi, people can focus their attention.
藉由打太極拳時集中精神於呼吸,注意力得以集中。

B 常說的話

To me, Tai Chi exercises might be a bit too slow.
對我而言,太極拳的練習可能有點太緩慢。

To me, Tai Chi does not look like a type of sport or martial art.
對我而言,太極拳看起來不像是一種運動或武術。

Most movements seem to be too gentle to be used in defense.
大部分動作似乎太溫柔而不能用於防禦。

I've been "Holding the Tree" for quite a while, and I feel nothing.
我已經「抱樹」有好一陣子了,而我完全沒感覺。

Somehow I can feel the "qi" inside of me, but I'm not able to control it.
我感到體內有一股氣,但是我沒辦法控制它。

What health benefits can Tai Chi bring to us?
太極拳對我們的健康有什麼好處?

Let's hope Tai Chi can promote balance control and general health.
但願太極拳能對平衡感和整體健康有幫助。

This Yang style Tai Chi can really help me deal with stress.
楊家太極真的能幫我緩解壓力。

Unit 2 Qi Gong
氣功

To me, Qi Gong can only happen in Gongfu movies.
對我而言,氣功只會在功夫片裡發生。

情境對話 1

A Do you want to go to "Introduction to Qi Gong" with me?
你想要和我一起去上「氣功入門課」嗎?

B First of all, what is Qi Gong?
首先我想問,什麼是氣功?

A You'll find out after this one hour session.
上完一小時的課後,你就會知道了。

B Is it hard for me to follow the instructions?
對我來說,課堂上的指示很難懂嗎?

A All you need to know is "inhale" and "exhale" in Chinese.
你只需要知道吸和呼的中文。

B I can see it is a sport about breathing and movements.
由此可知,氣功是關於呼吸和動作的運動。

情境對話 2

A Do you want to see a Qi Gong master perform?
你想要去看氣功師父表演嗎？

B Yes, I am very into that sort of Gongfu thing.
我想要，我對那種功夫的東西很感興趣。

A Why are you saying it is Gongfu?
為什麼你說那是功夫呢？

B To me, Qi Gong can only happen in Gongfu movies.
對我而言，氣功只會在功夫片裡發生。

A Sometimes I wonder how Qi Gong heals illnesses, too.
有時候我也在思考氣功怎麼醫治人。

B They say Qi Gong masters do not even have to touch the patient.
聽說氣功師父根本不需要接觸到病人。

A They can apply life energy with Qi Gong practices.
他們可以運氣給對方。

B Please ask the Qi Gong master to demonstrate for us.
請你要求師父表演給我們看。

Ⓐ 常說的話

Qi Gong is a powerful system of healing from China.
氣功是中國一種有效的醫療方式。

Qi Gong is about breathing, meditating and moving.
氣功和呼吸、靜坐以及動作有關。

The goal of Qi Gong is to circulate the life energy.
氣功的目的是為了使氣血流通。

Qi Gong leads to clearer state of mind and better health.
氣功可使人思想變清晰,健康變好。

Some practice Qi Gong as a way of non-contact treatment.
有些人藉由氣功來做不需接觸的治療。

Qi Gong can be spiritual and leads to self-awareness.
氣功可當作修行,增進自我意識。

Qi Gong practice can prevent illnesses and heal oneself.
氣功練習可預防疾病,自我療癒。

Qi Gong has a lot in common with Tai Chi.
氣功和太極有很多相似處。

Ⓑ 常說的話

Right breathing makes simple movements healing.
正確的呼吸使得簡單的動作有療效。

Many Qi Gong movements are a lot easier than Tai Chi.
很多氣功動作比太極簡單多。

Can Qi Gong really teach us how to react to stress better?
氣功真能教我們如何對付壓力?

How is Qi Gong used to heal diseases?
氣功是如何用來治病?

How can the life energy be transmitted with no contact?
沒有接觸,那麼氣是如何轉移的?

Qi Gong does not seem to follow physical laws.
氣功似乎不符合物理原則。

Some Qi Gong exercises can be very exhausting.
有些氣功練習非常累人。

How long does it take to become a Qi Gong master?
需要多久才能成為氣功大師?

Unit 3 Yoga 瑜珈

track 152

Yoga can improve health and reduce stress.
瑜珈能增進健康,減少壓力。

●情境對話 1

A I'm going to miss my yoga class.
我快要趕不上我的瑜珈課了。

B Don't rush for your yoga session.
不要衝著去上瑜珈課。

A It's hard to be always calm.
要隨時心平氣和很難。

B You are telling me.
這還用得著你告訴我。

A Why don't you come with me to my yoga school?
你何不和我一起去我的瑜珈學校看看?

B That sounds like a good idea.
這個主意聽起來很好。

情境對話 2

A Did you learn yoga in the States?
你在美國練過瑜珈嗎?

B I've only watched others practicing yoga.
我只有看過別人練瑜珈。

A Do you want to join us in the yoga session?
你想要加入我們的瑜珈課嗎?

B Can you tell me what benefit yoga has brought to you?
你可不可以告訴我瑜珈帶給你什麼好處?

A My back pain has improved very much.
我的背痛改善了很多。

B Have you lost a lot of weight?
你瘦了很多嗎?

A No, not really, but my purpose of doing yoga is to stay fit.
這倒沒有,不過我練瑜珈的目的是為了保持健康。

B You look really fit.
你看來真的很健康。

ⓐ常說的話

Recently yoga has become very popular in Taiwan.
近來瑜珈在台灣變得很風行。

Some of the yoga teachers come from India.
有些瑜珈老師來自印度。

Yoga students include both females and males.
瑜珈學生包括女性和男性。

The yoga students work on several postures of yoga together.
瑜珈學生一起練習好幾個瑜珈姿勢。

There are some special yoga classes, such as, for pregnant women.
有一些特殊的瑜珈課程,例如開給懷孕女性的課。

Down Dog Pose is one of the postures we often practice.
下犬式是我們常練習的姿勢之一。

Tree Pose can work on the balance of the body.
樹式可以訓練身體平衡。

Some poses are easy, but some are really tough to do.
有些姿勢很容易,有些真的很難做到。

track 跨頁共同導讀 153

B 常說的話

Why do you breathe deeply in Lotus Pose in the beginning?
為什麼你們在開始時要做蓮花座並深呼吸?

Some postures look easy but are hard to practice.
有些姿勢看來容易,但非常難做。

Many of the yoga postures look like animal poses.
很多瑜珈姿勢看來像動物姿勢。

It's hard to take care of breathing while doing yoga poses.
做瑜珈姿勢時還要注意呼吸是很困難的。

All of the yoga teachers here look slim and fit.
這裡的所有瑜珈老師看起來苗條又健康。

How long will it take me to be as good as the yoga teacher?
我要花多久時間才可以做得像瑜珈老師那麼好?

Can this yoga exercise really make my spine supple?
這個瑜珈真的能讓我的脊椎變柔軟嗎?

Have you heard of yoga in the water?
你聽過水中瑜珈嗎?

Unit 4 Spa 水療

Every morning I go to the spa for an hour.
每天早晨我做一小時的水療。

●情境對話 1

A Do you want to go to the spa?
你想要去做水療嗎？

B Is it very expensive?
會很貴嗎？

A We are going to a community health center.
我們去的是社區健康中心。

B Do they have swimming pools with spa facilities there?
那邊有附有水療設施的游泳池嗎？

A That's right, and the entry ticket doesn't cost very much.
對，而且門票非常便宜。

B I'm going with you!
我跟你一起去！

情境對話 2

A The spa feels like massage for the back.
這個水療感覺起來像是背部的按摩。

B The flows are neither too strong nor too weak.
水流不會太強也不會太弱。

A To me, it is a lazy way of exercise muscles.
對我來說,這是種懶人練肌肉的方法。

B That's exactly what I feel like.
那正是我的感覺。

A Do you want to try other types of spa?
你想要試試看其它種類的水療嗎?

B Not now. I feel like staying here forever.
不是現在。我想要永遠待在這裡。

A Come on. Let others have the chance to try this one, too.
別這樣,讓別人也有機會試試這個。

B Okay. Let's go to the cool pool together.
好,我們一起去冷池。

Ⓐ常說的話●

Have you tried all types of the spa in the pool?
你試過池內所有種類的水療了嗎?

Watch out for your neck because the water is quite strong.
小心你的頸部,因為這水注很強。

The elderly can come to the spa for free in the morning.
早上年長者可以免費來這裡做水療。

What areas of your muscles are especially sore?
你的肌肉哪部分特別痠?

Look, the bubbles keep coming out of the wall!
你看,泡泡不斷從牆上冒出!

You seem to like to have water coming down from above.
你似乎喜歡水從上面沖下來。

I like to switch from the hot pool to the cold one and back and forth.
我喜歡從熱池到冷池不斷交替著泡。

After doing spa, I usually swim a few laps in the swimming pool.
做完水療後,我通常去泳池游個幾圈。

B 常說的話

This is really a special treat for my sore muscles.
這對我痠痛的肌肉真算是種特別的款待。

Wouldn't it be even better if we didn't have to wear swimsuits?
要是我們不用穿泳衣該有多好。

They even have small pools for children and little children.
他們還有給小孩和小小孩的小池。

That water from above seems a bit too strong for me.
從上面沖下的水注對我來說似乎太強了。

The water coming from the ground can massage my feet.
從地下冒出的水可以按摩我的腳。

The spa that can massage the lower back is popular.
可以按摩下背部的水療很受歡迎。

The water is so strong that I am floating.
這水這麼強,我都浮起來了。

If we stay too long, we might get sore muscles from the spa.
如果我們待太久,我們可能會因水療而肌肉痠痛。

Unit 5 Chinese Medicine
中醫

Traditional Chinese medicine is very popular nowadays.
傳統中醫現在很受歡迎。

●情境對話1●

A I've got a bad headache.
我的頭好痛。

B Why don't you take an aspirin?
你怎麼不吃顆阿斯匹林呢?

A Usually I drink ginger tea to get rid of a headache.
通常我喝薑母茶舒緩頭痛。

B People say many plants are used in Chinese medicine.
聽說很多植物被用來作中藥。

A Herbal medicine works very well.
草藥的功效非常好。

B It must be very gentle.
想必很溫和。

情境對話 2

A What happened to your right knee?
你的右膝蓋怎麼了?

B I got hurt playing tennis this afternoon.
今天下午我打網球時受傷了。

A I can take you to Dr. Chen, our acupuncturist.
我可以帶你去看陳醫師,他是我們的針灸醫師。

B How horrible would it be to have needles in my body!
在身體上插針,那多恐怖!

A Dr. Chen is very experienced, and you wouldn't feel anything.
陳醫師很有經驗,你不會有任何感覺的。

B I suppose I should "do in Rome as the Romans do."
我想我應該入境隨俗。

A Dr. Chen will also prescribe herbal medicine for you.
陳醫師也會為你開中藥服用。

B I'll try anything to get well soon.
為了能早日康復,我什麼都願意試。

Ⓐ 常說的話

Chinese medicine regards a person as a whole being.
中醫視人為一個整體。

Chinese medicine does not treat one symptom at a time.
中醫不會一次只治療一個症狀。

Chinese medicine may be used to strengthen one's general health.
中醫可以用來加強一個人的整體健康。

Many women who cannot have children seek help from Chinese medicine.
很多不能懷孕的婦女尋求中醫的幫助。

Many ingredients of food have medical purposes in Chinese medicine.
很多食物的食材在中醫上有醫療效果。

Acupuncture is not as terrible as you probably imagine.
針灸不像你可能想的那樣恐怖。

Even little children do not have problems with acupuncture.
即使是很小的小孩子對針灸也不會有問題。

Some prefer Chinese medicine to western medicine because of fewer side effects.
有些人比較喜歡中醫,因為相較於西醫,中醫的副作用較少。

track 跨頁共同導讀 157

Ⓑ 常說的話

Does acupuncture have a scientific basis?
針灸有科學根據嗎?

In the States, more and more patients go to Chinese medicine clinics.
在美國,越來越多人到中醫診所就醫。

What are they doing with those glass bottles on his back?
他背上的那些玻璃杯是用來做什麼的?

What is the herb that the doctor is burning?
那位醫師在燒什麼草藥?

Chinese medicine seems to be herbs and dried bones to me.
中藥對我來說似乎是草藥和乾骨。

The doctor mixed many herbs for my prescription.
那位醫師混了很多的草藥,作為我的處方。

Chinese medicine tastes really bitter to me.
對我而言,中藥嚐起來真的很苦。

Are they serious about making this into Chinese medicine?
他們真的要把這個做成中藥嗎?

Unit 6 Massage 按摩

Massage is good to your health.
按摩對你的健康很好。

●情境對話1●

A Come with me to have a massage!
一起和我去按摩!

B I don't seem to have any problems with my body.
我的身體似乎沒有任何問題。

A Your muscles are often too tense.
你的肌肉常常太緊張。

B Can a massage help me unwind?
按摩可以幫我放鬆嗎?

A Of course. These blind masseurs are very professional.
當然。這些視障按摩師非常專業。

B They must be really good.
他們一定很厲害。

跟老外介紹台灣這本全包了

track 跨頁共同導讀 158

●情境對話2●

A There is one foot massage salon near your hostel.
你的旅社附近有家腳底按摩店。

B Why do they give the foot special massage?
為什麼要給腳部特別的按摩呢?

A They believe the reflex points of the foot connect with all organs.
他們相信腳底的反射點和內臟相連。

B Is that why they stimulate different parts of the foot?
那就是為什麼他們要刺激腳的不同部位嗎?

A They have special hand techniques.
他們有特別的手法。

B Why do they soak our feet in salt water first?
為什麼他們要先把我們的腳浸在鹽水?

A This is to make sure our feet are clean before massage.
這是為了要確定我們的腳在按摩前很乾淨。

B All of these things are totally new to me.
這些對我全都是新奇的事物。

Ⓐ 常說的話

Many people have foot massages regularly in Taiwan.
在台灣很多人定期做腳底按摩。

A good massage can relax your head, neck, shoulders and arms.
好的按摩可以放鬆你的頭部、頸部、肩膀和手臂。

Usually customers are required to lie on special beds for massage.
客人通常會被要求躺在特別的床上接受按摩。

Many blind masseurs are trained massage experts.
很多視障的按摩師是經過專業訓練的按摩專家。

Massage is part of many physical therapies.
按摩是很多物理治療的一部分。

Ⓑ 常說的話

Lately I come across several Thai massage salons in Taipei.
最近我在台北看到好幾家泰式按摩店。

I bought a book to teach myself massage, but it didn't work out.
我買了一本按摩書來自學,但是沒有用。

Chapter 12

Returning
回國

Unit 1 Checking out of the Hotel
飯店退房

What time are you going to check out of the hotel?
你幾點要退房？

●情境對話 1●

A What time are you going to check out of the hotel this morning?
今早你幾點要退房？

B I'm going to check out in a minute.
我等一下就要退房。

A You'd better do a complete check of your room first.
你最好先徹底檢查一下你的房間。

B Thank you for reminding me.
謝謝你提醒我。

A Did you have any special service?
你有點了什麼特別的服務嗎？

B No, but I drank some cans of beer in the minibar.
沒有，但是我喝了幾罐小冰箱裡的啤酒。

情境對話 2

A Please check out of the hotel before eleven o'clock next morning.
請在明早十一點前退房。

B I can do that, no problem.
這個我沒問題。

A Please check the bill before you sign it.
在簽名前請檢查帳單。

B Could there be any mistakes?
會有錯誤嗎?

A Usually not, but sometimes mistakes can happen.
通常不會有,但有時錯誤可能發生。

B This time I only stayed in this hotel for three nights.
這次我只在這個飯店住了三晚。

A Did you have any room services?
你點了什麼客房服務嗎?

B Only meal-ordering service and laundry service.
只有送餐服務和洗衣服務。

A 常說的話

Have you checked all of the items on the bill?
你檢查過了帳單上所有項目了嗎?

Please check every item on the bill before signing it.
在簽名前請檢查帳單上所有項目。

This is the repairing service on your bill.
你的帳單上有這麼一項修理服務。

Did you have your breakfast delivered to the room?
你是否有請他們把早餐送到房間?

Please check the room carefully before you return the key.
歸還鑰匙前請仔細檢查房間。

Did you have any of the beverages from the minibar?
你有拿小冰箱裡的飲料嗎?

Take your time, we are in no hurry.
慢慢來,我們不急。

There is a good souvenir shop in the hotel.
這家飯店有很好的紀念品店。

❸ 常說的話

Should I leave a tip when I check out the room?
退房時我該留下小費嗎?

I don't remember if I ordered breakfast room service.
我不記得是否點了早餐的送餐服務。

I don't think I watched any pay-per-view movies.
我想我沒有看付費電影。

The bill does not look quite accurate to me.
帳單看起來不太對勁。

The bill is more than I thought.
帳單上的價錢比我想的還高。

The service of the hotel is outstanding.
這家飯店的服務很不錯。

Can the hotel staff order a taxi for me?
飯店的員工可以為我叫輛計程車嗎?

Are the taxi drivers here willing to take me to the airport?
這裡的計程車司機會願意載我去機場嗎?

Unit 2 Buying Souvenirs
買紀念品

What should I buy to give to my family as souvenirs?
我該給我的家人買什麼紀念品呢？

●情境對話1

A Do you want to go gift shopping for your family?
你想要為你家人買些紀念品禮品嗎？

B I see the advertisements for pineapple cake everywhere.
我到處看到鳳梨酥的廣告。

A Does your family like sweets?
你的家人喜歡甜食嗎？

B They sure do.
他們很喜歡。

A If so, pineapple cake is a good choice.
這樣的話，鳳梨酥是個好主意。

B Can you help me choose which pineapple cakes to buy?
你能幫我選擇該買哪種鳳梨酥？

跟老外介紹台灣這本全包了

track 跨頁共同導讀 162

●情境對話 2

A What do you want to buy as souvenirs from Taiwan?
你想要買什麼當台灣的紀念品？

B The cultural and creative industries are very popular now.
文創產業現在很流行。

A In recent years indigenous design attracts lots of attention.
近年來原住民設計吸引了很多人的注意力。

B Do you mean works by indigenous artists?
你的意思是原住民藝術家的作品？

A Sometimes it's hard to tell if it is really indigenous works of art.
有時候很難辨別是否真的是原住民藝術作品。

B Are you saying non-indigenous artists pretend to be indigenous?
你是說有冒牌的原住民藝術家？

A That happens, and besides, many indigenous artists move to the cities.
有那樣的情形，另外，很多原住民藝術家搬到城市。

B I think all cultures now are influenced by other cultures.
我想現在所有的文化都受到其它文化的影響。

350

ⒶA常說的話●

You can taste all pastries here before you buy.
這裡的糕餅在買前都可以試吃。

I like to eat pineapple cake and drink tea.
我喜歡一邊吃鳳梨酥一邊喝茶。

I can take you to a pastry shop if you like.
如果你有興趣,我可以帶你到一家糕餅店。

Do you have somebody in mind when you shop for gifts?
你在買禮物時,心裡會想著要給誰嗎?

This earring is a product of the cultural and creative industry.
這個耳環是個文創產品。

This indigenous painting is a suitable gift for your family.
這幅原住民的畫作為你家人的禮物很合適。

The small indigenous woven bags can be good souvenirs.
這些原住民的小織包可以當作不錯的紀念品。

Chopsticks can be interesting gifts for westerners.
筷子可以作為給西方人的有趣禮物。

❸ 常說的話

Could you please take me to a duty-free store?
你可以帶我去免稅商店嗎？

This pineapple cake with tea flavor tastes fantastic.
這個帶有茶味的鳳梨酥真好吃。

Do most Taiwanese like pineapple cake?
大部分的台灣人喜歡鳳梨酥嗎？

My elder brother would like this T-shirt with the dragon.
我哥哥會喜歡這件印有龍的 T 恤。

Would chopsticks from the supermarket make a good gift?
超級市場的筷子可以當作是好禮送人嗎？

I think my aunt would like this small silk purse.
我想我的姑姑會喜歡這個小絲包。

I like handicraft because it is hand-made and unique.
我喜歡手工藝品，因為那是手工做的，也很獨特。

What does the cultural and creative industry mean exactly?
請問文創產業確切的意思是什麼？

Unit 3 Expressing Gratitude
感謝

Thank you for showing me around.
謝謝你帶我到處參觀。

情境對話 1

A Are you all set for your return trip?
你準備好了要搭機回去了嗎?

B Yes, I am all ready.
我都準備好了。

A I hope you have a safe flight.
祝你旅途平安。

B Can I buy you a drink to thank you?
我可以請你喝杯飲料來謝謝你嗎?

A Can I buy you a pearl milk tea in return?
那我可以回請你喝杯珍珠奶茶嗎?

B It's a deal.
就這麼說定了。

跟老外介紹台灣這本全包了

track 跨頁共同導讀 164

●情境對話 2

Ⓐ Don't go to bed too late.
可不要太晚睡覺。

Ⓑ Why does my flight have to be so early in the morning?
為什麼我的班機得要這麼早呢？

Ⓐ Call me if there's any problem at the airport.
如果在機場有任何問題，打電話給我。

Ⓑ Thank you, but there shouldn't be any problem.
謝謝，但是應該不會有任何問題。

Ⓐ I'd like to give you this picture of Buddha to keep.
我想要給你這張佛像作保留。

Ⓑ Oh, that's very thoughtful of you.
哦，你真是非常體貼。

Ⓐ You mentioned that sometimes you feel a little airsick.
你說過你有時會有點暈機。

Ⓑ I'll take this picture with me. Thank you for your kindness.
我會帶著這張佛卡。謝謝你的好意。

Ⓐ常說的話

It was my pleasure to show you around.
能帶你到處參觀,是我的榮幸。

I enjoyed visiting scenic spots with you.
我很開心能和你一起參觀景點。

I am the one who should say thank you.
我才該謝謝你。

I enjoyed your company, too.
我也很喜歡和你在一起。

Because of you, I made it to Orchid Island.
因為你,我到了蘭嶼一趟。

Please come again next time.
請下次再來。

Next time please stay longer in Taiwan.
下次請待在台灣久一點。

Bring your friends next time!
下次帶你的朋友來!

ⓑ 常說的話

Thank you for your great hospitality.
謝謝你的盛情款待。

I really appreciate you showing me around in Taiwan.
我真的很感謝你帶我參觀台灣。

You are a wonderful tour guide.
你是位很好的導遊。

I really can't thank you enough.
我真的不知道怎麼感謝你。

You helped me very much in organizing hostels.
你在安排旅社方面,幫了我很大的忙。

How I wish we could have more time!
要是我們能有更多的時間,該有多好!

Thank you for spending so much time with me.
謝謝你花了這麼多時間陪我。

Please visit me in the States, so I can show you around.
請來美國拜訪我,這樣我才能帶你到處玩。

Unit 4 Final Farewells
最後道別

I'll come to Taiwan again very soon.
我很快就會再來台灣。

情境對話 1

A Do you need a lift to the airport?
你需要我載你去機場嗎?

B No need because I can take a bus to the airport.
不需要,因為我可以搭客運到機場。

A Always ask for directions if you get lost.
如果你迷路了,就跟別人問路。

B Thank you for all you've done for me.
謝謝你為我做的一切。

A You are always welcome to Taiwan.
隨時歡迎你來台灣。

B Next time I'll bring my parents with me to Taiwan.
下次我會帶我的父母一起來台灣。

跟老外介紹台灣這本全包了

track 跨頁共同導讀 166

●情境對話2

🅐 When is your next visit to Taiwan?
你下次什麼時候來台灣？

🅑 I'm applying for a Chinese course for next summer.
我正在申請明年夏天的中文課程。

🅐 That is a very wise decision.
那是個明智的決定。

🅑 In a year we can see each other again.
再過一年我們就可以再見面了。

🅐 Invite your parents to visit Taiwan while you study Chinese here.
趁你在這裡學中文時，邀請你的父母來台灣玩。

🅑 They would be very glad to visit me in Taiwan.
他們會很高興來台灣找我。

🅐 I'd be glad to show you and your parents around in Taiwan.
我會很樂意帶你和你父母參觀台灣。

🅑 I appreciate all you've done for me.
我很感謝你為我所做的一切。

Ⓐ常說的話

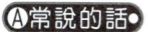

Write me an E-mail after you arrive in Seattle safely.
安全到達西雅圖後,寫封電子郵件給我。

Do you usually suffer from jet lag?
你通常有時差問題嗎?

I have the feeling very soon we'll see each other again.
我有種感覺,很快我們就會再見面。

You can always ask me for help if you need anything.
如果你需要什麼幫忙,都可以找我。

Ⓑ 常說的話

We can start to plan our trip in Taiwan next time.
我們可以開始計畫下次的台灣之旅。

We can chat online if you don't mind the time difference.
如果你不介意時差,我們可以在網路上聊天。

I'm lucky to have come across someone like you in Taiwan.
我很幸運在台灣遇到像你這樣的人。

Let me know if you have the chance to visit the U.S.
如果你有機會來美國玩,請通知我。

雅典文化

QR Code
雅典英研所 企編
(附QR Code隨掃隨聽音檔)

Everyday English

說明　情境對話1　情境對話2　字彙

天天一句
生活英語

萬裡挑一! 讓你再也不會
怎麼辦怎麼辦的
菜英文.基礎實用篇

我是英語會話王

報復性旅遊必備的
旅遊英語

菜英文
生活應用篇

雲端mp3.mp4.
QR Code

無敵英語會話王

無敵英語單字王

最直覺的英文文法

生活單字萬用手冊

生活句型萬用手冊

生活英語萬用手冊

永續圖書
線上購物網

www.foreverbooks.com.tw

◆ 加入會員即享活動及會員折扣。
◆ 每月均有優惠活動，期期不同。
◆ 新加入會員三天內訂購書籍不限本數金額，
　即贈送精選書籍一本。（依網站標示為主）

專業圖書發行、書局經銷、圖書出版

永續圖書總代理：
五觀藝術出版社、培育文化、棋茵出版社、犬拓文化、讀品文化、雅典文化、大億文化、璞申文化、智學堂文化、語言鳥文化

活動期內，永續圖書將保留變更或終止該活動之權利及最終決定權。